Muslim
in
Pitfalls and Pranks

by

Maryam Mahmoodian

MUSLIM WRITERS PUBLISHING
TEMPE, ARIZONA

Published by Muslim Writers Publishing
P.O. Box 27362
Tempe, Arizona. 85285
USA

www.MuslimWritersPublishing.com

Library of Congress Catalog Control Number: 2007943048
ISBN 978-0-9793577-3-2

Cover art by Shirley Gavin
Book cover and layout design by Leila Joiner
Editing by Pamela K. Taylor

Printed in the United States of America

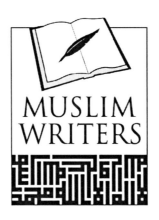

MUSLIM
WRITERS

Muslim Teens
in
Pitfalls and Pranks

Acknowledgements

Thanks to my parents who always encouraged me to write.

And special thanks to a young Iraqi girl named Zaynab who inspired the character of Elham and whose difficulties led me to the idea of the book to begin with.

Chapter 1

FOURTEEN-YEAR-OLD ELHAM ALAMERY sighed as she stood by her locker after school gathering up her books. She loved her challenging classes, but despised all the homework that came with them. She had closed her locker and was starting to turn around when she heard a girl's voice behind her.

"Look! It's Bin Laden's twin, Elham," the girl said, and then several other students laughed.

Elham turned around cautiously. Because she was one of the few Muslim girls in public school who wore the hijab (or head scarf), she had endured taunting and teasing throughout her school years. However, up to that point, high school had been much better than either elementary school or junior high.

"Hi, Elham bin Laden," one of the girls said tauntingly.

"Be careful," another girl added, "maybe she'll blow us up."

Elham closed her locker and tried to control her temper. "Excuse me," she said. "I need to go find my brother." A crowd of students had gathered around them, and she hated being the center of attention, especially this kind of attention.

"You mean your brother Saddam Hussein?" the first girl said.

"My brother's name is Khalid, and I hate Saddam!" Elham said hotly.

"What? Did you say you love Saddam? Elham loves Saddam? So why don't you go back to Iraq and stay with him in jail? Maybe he'll marry you."

"Yeah, Saddam and Elham Hussein," another girl said, puckering up her lips and making kiss noises.

"Stop it!" Elham shouted, trying to work her way through the crowd of kids. Just then one of the girls pushed her, and she fell down, hitting her arm and shoulder against the lockers. With that, Elham became really angry. She stood up and shoved the girl back, making her bang into the lockers just as their science teacher walked by.

"Elham!" Mrs. Falls exclaimed. "Stop that!" She pulled Elham away. "Get your books. We're going to the principal's office."

The ringleader of the gang of students smirked at Elham.

"But she pushed me first," Elham protested, pointing at the girl who had knocked her down. She was still standing right next to the lockers.

"I didn't see it. It's none of my business." Mrs. Falls grabbed Elham's arm more tightly. "I'll let the principal deal with you if he thinks it's needed," she added to the other girl, and then firmly led Elham away. "You know, this is exactly what I would expect from someone like you. The only thing you and your people know how to do is resort to violence."

"I didn't resort to violence," Elham said furiously. "She's the one that started it."

"Yeah, yeah, of course." As they entered the principal's office, Mrs. Falls loosened her grip on Elham's wrist.

"What's going on?" the secretary asked.

"I found her pushing another student," Mrs. Falls told her. "The other girl was Kathy Mills."

"Where is she?"

"I didn't bring her," Mrs. Falls admitted.

"Why not?"

"Because I was too busy with this one."

"What's your name?" the secretary asked Elham.

"Elham AlAmery," she replied.

"Have a seat. I'll tell Mr. Kinzey you're here." The secretary disappeared.

Elham glanced around her. There were two other students also waiting for the principal. One was a dark-haired boy wearing all black. The other was another dark-haired boy with blue bangs. She looked down at the floor nervously. She had never been in trouble before.

After what seemed like forever, Mr. Kinzey finally appeared in the waiting area. "Did you page the other girl?" he asked his secretary.

"Yes, I did. She still isn't here yet."

"Elham?" he said pleasantly. "Come on back with me."

"Will it take long? I have to meet my brother, Khalid."

"Page Khalid AlAmery," Mr. Kinzey instructed the secretary. He turned back to Elham. "Is that okay?"

She nodded and dutifully followed the principal back to his office. He closed the door and sat down at his desk. She sat in one of the chairs that was in front of it.

"Elham AlAmery," Mr. Kinzey said. "We were just talking about you."

Elham's eyes widened when she heard him say that. She was really surprised because she had never been in trouble before.

"Yes," he continued. "Mr. Collins was saying you're one of his best students." Mr. Collins was her English teacher. "He said when you read *The Pearl*, none of the other kids took it seriously, but you understood it right away and wrote one of the best reviews he's ever read." He paused. "So what happened today?" he asked gently.

"They were teasing me," Elham said quietly. "And the one girl—I don't even know her name—she pushed me. So I pushed her back."

"Why were they teasing you?"

"Because I'm Muslim. They were calling me Elham bin Laden, and they said I love Saddam Hussein. And they called my brother Khalid—they called him Saddam. I hate Saddam. He killed my grandfather and my uncle. Why would they say that?" Tears welled up in her eyes.

"Maybe they don't know about your family."

She sniffed. "They don't care."

"Even so, it's never okay to fight." Mr. Kinzey sighed. "I'm sure you know that. But since this is your first time, I'm not going to punish you. I do need to call your parents, though."

"No, please," she pleaded. "Please don't call them. They'll get really upset. Please, I would rather go to detention or whatever."

"I have to," he insisted. "Do you want to be here when I talk to them? Or you can go ahead and go. I had my secretary page your brother, so he should be waiting for you."

"I'll go." She stood up. "I can't listen. Why do you have to call them?"

"It's our policy," he said gently. "But I'm just going to tell them exactly what you told me. Oh, and Elham? I will talk to the other girl, too. Mrs. Falls should have brought her down here with you."

"Mrs. Falls hates me," Elham said bitterly. "Yesterday she asked me if I consider myself an American. And just now she said that all my people know how to do is violence."

"Did she? When did she say that about being an American?" Mr. Kinzey demanded.

"Yesterday after class. I was standing at her desk to give her my homework. We were the last people, me and Alexis. And she said that 'cause Alexis is Muslim, too. But she doesn't cover her hair."

"Hmm… anyway." He smiled. "Go on home. I'll see you to-morrow."

Elham left the office and sat back down in one of the chairs to wait for her brother.

~

Meanwhile, down the hallway, fifteen-year-old Ibrahim Karim was gathering his books at his locker when he heard a familiar voice behind him.

"I still don't understand the biology assignment," the girl was saying. "Let's ask Ibrahim. He's smart. He'll understand it."

Ibrahim turned around to find two popular sophomore girls walking up to him.

"Hey, Ibrahim," one of them said, twirling a piece of her blonde hair.

"Hey, Christy," he replied casually.

"Do you understand the biology assignment from today?" she asked him. "Science is so hard for me."

Before he could say anything, they were interrupted by a page overhead. "Kathy Mills, please report to the principal's office im-mediately. Kathy Mills, please report to the principal's office."

"It's not that hard," he said.

"Well, maybe you can explain it to me, then," she suggested flirtatiously. "Do you have time?"

"You mean, like, now?"

She shrugged. "Yeah, why not?"

"Well, my friend's waiting for me, to give me a ride home," he told her.

"Well, can you call me?" Christy asked. She wrote her tele-phone number down on a piece of paper and handed it to him. "Call me, okay? I don't want to fail."

Ibrahim smiled. "You won't. See you later." He began walking away and almost ran right into his best friend, Khalid AlAmery, a junior.

"Hey, what's up?" Ibrahim said, trying to sound casual.

"Nothing. What's up with you?"

"Nothing."

Just then the overhead page began again. "Khalid AlAmery, please report to the principal's office. Khalid AlAmery, please report to the principal's office."

"What?" Khalid said in surprise. "What's going on?"

"Is everything okay?" Ibrahim asked.

"I think so. I don't know. I'd better go. I still need to find Elham and Hafsa." Hafsa was a friend of Elham's who lived near them. They drove her to and from school every day. As Khalid hurried away, he called back to Ibrahim, "Call me tonight!"

Khalid walked quickly to the principal's office. He hoped everything was okay. He had never been paged there before. As he approached the door, he saw Hafsa waiting outside.

"I heard the page, so I thought I would just meet you here," she told him.

They went inside together and found Elham sitting in the waiting area. She jumped up when she saw them.

"What happened?" Khalid asked her.

"Nothing," Elham said sullenly. "Let's go."

The parking lot was half empty since most of the students had already left. Elham climbed in the back seat next to Hafsa, instead of sitting in front like normal. Khalid took advantage of the empty parking lot to back up and pull out faster than usual. As they rushed over a speed bump, even with their seatbelts on, Hafsa and Elham bounced up.

"Khalid!" Elham grouchily reprimanded.

"Sorry," he said quickly.

"You should be," she grumbled from the backseat.

Khalid pulled out of the parking lot and ran through a yellow light that took them onto the main road going home. Normally Elham would ignore Khalid's slightly hazardous driving, but today she spoke up.

"Khalid, you really should be more careful," she chided.

"Oh, I'm sorry," Khalid apologized as he passed a slow-moving car. "Does my driving make you nervous?"

Elham rolled her eyes from the backseat. "Why wouldn't it?" she mumbled under her breath.

"Well, I would kind of like to make it home all in one piece," Hafsa replied, sounding only half-joking.

Khalid and Hafsa could see that something was bothering Elham and tried to keep her spirits up by bantering back and forth about school and his erratic driving. Normally Elham would pitch in to the conversation. However, that day, she was quiet the whole way home. All she could think about was the moment when she would enter her house and have to face her mother, and then later her father.

Because both of Elham's parents had grown up in Iraq, they didn't understand what it was like to be a teenager in the United States. Although they tried to push their children to do well in school, it was not so easy. Mr. AlAmery had just graduated from high school when he was drafted to join the Iraqi military to fight in the war with Iran. He had served during almost the entire eight-year war. He often felt that he could have gone on to college if his family had had the money to get him out of military service. Mrs. AlAmery had quit high school to help her parents at home. She was the youngest daughter in her family and did not marry until her mid-twenties which was quite old for her village. After the first Gulf War, they had joined the revolution against Saddam Hussain. When it was crushed, they were forced to flee into neighboring Saudi Arabia where they spent several years in a refugee camp before being granted asylum in the US. Perhaps it was because of the difficult lives her parents had lived that they pushed their children to do well in school and to not make trouble.

Elham had had her share of trouble in school, though, especially during the last two years in junior high. She had started wearing hijab in fifth grade, shortly before September 11. In the beginning, she endured mostly questions, but after September 11, things took a turn for the worse. In junior high, she was one of a handful of girls who wore hijab, including Hafsa and her two other best friends, Nur and Nadia. They had all shared similar experiences of taunting and teasing from other students. Nur had been one of the best girls' basketball players in their last year of junior high, but she refused to play in high school (despite the coaches' urging) because of all the taunting she had endured after games when she wore her hijab and sweatpants.

Elham sighed as Khalid pulled into their driveway. He looked over at her sympathetically. "It'll be okay, Ellie," he told her. "Whatever happened, I'm sure it wasn't your fault."

Elham started crying. "I'm never going back to school again," she said. She opened the car door, grabbed her backpack, and ran into the house where her mother was waiting.

Mrs. AlAmery hugged her sobbing daughter. "It's okay, Ellie. Don't cry," she consoled her.

"I'm sorry, mama," Elham cried. "It wasn't my fault."

"I know. It's okay. Azizi, I'm not mad."

"Do we have to tell Baba? Please don't tell him," she pleaded.

Mrs. AlAmery led Elham over to the couch as Khalid entered the house and quietly disappeared into his bedroom.

"Ellie, azizi, it's okay. He's not going to be mad. I talked to Mr. Kinzey. We know it wasn't your fault."

"I don't want to go back to school," Elham declared.

"I know, honey. I know. But there's nothing we can do about that. You have to."

"Why? Please don't make me."

"You can't run away from your problems and expect that they'll go away," her mother said. "You just have to know that you are so lucky. You've had so many problems and experiences in your life, and you always survive. That's why you're so strong now."

Elham sniffed. "I've never had problems like this before."

"Sure you have," Mrs. AlAmery told her. "For one, you were born five weeks early and during a war. We couldn't even take you to the hospital. And when you were only a month old, you survived days of horrible conditions, so we could get across the border into Saudi Arabia. You lived almost six years in that refugee camp where kids around you were getting sick and even dying, and you survived. Then you came here and learned English and went to school and now look. You're in high school. You have A's in all of your classes. Mr. Kinzey said your English teacher thinks you're one of his best students. And you have friends and your family. You speak two languages. You've lived in three different countries. Elham, these girls are nothing compared to you."

"But I don't know why they have to be so mean. They called Khalid Saddam."

"I know. Mr. Kinzey said that seemed to bother you more than anything. He seems like a nice man," her mother said.

"He's okay."

"Anyway, don't worry about your dad. I'll talk to him, and he'll understand."

"Do we have to tell him?"

"Yes, of course. He's your father."

"But he'll just get angry with me."

"No, he won't, azizi. Believe me, he won't be."

"I don't want to be here when you tell him."

"Okay, I'll tell him tonight after you sleep," her mother promised. "Now, why don't you go pray and get changed. And then maybe you can help Nur with her term paper. Rana was telling me yesterday that she's having a hard time with it, and I know you like to write."

Nur Karim was one of Elham's best friends. She was one year younger than her brother Ibrahim, and like Elham was in the freshman class. Her mom, Rana, had been good friends with Elham's mom for a long time.

Elham smiled for the first time since she had come home from school. "Okay," she agreed. "Can you call her while I pray?"

"Sure."

They stood up and separated. Elham headed back to her bedroom, and Mrs. AlAmery went to the telephone to call the Karims. As Elham changed into more comfortable clothes, she imagined her petite mother, barely five feet tall and a hundred pounds, running through the desert with her husband, carrying their two very young children, trying to escape southern Iraq. She imagined the telephone call in Saudi Arabia when she received the news that her older brother had disappeared and presumably been killed by the former Iraqi regime. Elham's uncle was only two years older than her mother. Elham couldn't imagine what she would do if she was in a different country when she got the news that something had happened to Khalid, especially if she was unable to return home.

As tough as her troubles might seem, they were nothing compared to what her mom had gone through. Still she couldn't help thinking, "I hope I can get through this. I hope I can be as strong as my mom was."

Chapter 2

OVER AT THE KARIMS' HOUSE that evening, Ibrahim was sitting alone in the bedroom that he shared with his older brother, Saad. Saad was a freshman in college who also worked part-time at the local Blake Brothers Bookstore.

As Ibrahim began working on his English homework, he debated whether to call Christy, the girl who had stopped by his locker that afternoon. He was really tempted to, especially since Saad would be at work until 9:00 PM that night, so he had their bedroom all to himself. He could hear Nur and Elham talking next door. For the past year, Ibrahim had been almost infatuated with the idea of being a member of the "popular" crowd in his class. He also really wanted to have a girlfriend. It seemed like all of the popular guys had really cool girlfriends. Of course, Christy, being one of the cheerleaders, hung out with that group of kids.

After fifteen minutes of unfocused reading, he decided to make the call. He went out to let his parents know and found them talking in the kitchen.

"Hey, Mom, Dad, is it okay if I use your phone? I want to call Ali," he said. Ali Hussain was one of his friends. He was one year younger than Ibrahim.

"Sure. Is there some reason you don't want to use the phone in the family room?" Mr. Karim asked.

"Well…" His mind scrambled for a reply. "If Nur hears me, she'll interrupt us so she can talk to Nadia." Nadia was Ali's older sister.

His father shrugged. "Okay. Don't be on too long."

Ibrahim walked into his parents' bedroom and then took the cordless phone into his own room. After closing the door and laying back down on the bed, he quickly dialed the phone number before he lost his nerve.

"Hello," said the girl at the other end.

"Hi, is this Christy?" he asked.

"Ibrahim? Of course, it's me. This is my own private cell phone."

Wow, Ibrahim thought, she's got her own cell phone.

Aloud, he said, "Great. So what's up?"

"Nothing. What's up with you?" she replied.

"Well, I'm just trying to do some English. I have a lot of reading to do for that class."

"I'm sure it's easy for you. You're so smart. I bet you have an A in biology without even trying."

"So do you still need help with that?" Ibrahim asked her.

"Kind of. But I don't really care about biology. I'll do okay in it. Mrs. King likes me. I really just wanted to talk to you," Christy said.

Ibrahim could almost picture her, sitting in her bedroom, talking on her cell phone. He hoped none of her friends were there with her. "So what do you want to talk about?" he asked, trying to sound casual.

"Our date. When's it going to be?"

"What date? Did I ask you on a date?"

"No, but I'm asking you. I really like you, Ibrahim. I want to go out with you sometime," she said.

"Like when?" he replied.

"Like tomorrow if you want."

"Maybe after we get back from Thanksgiving vacation," Ibrahim said. "Because tomorrow's our last day this week."

"Okay, well do you want to come to a party this Friday night? One of my brother's friends is having one at his house. We can go together if you want."

"I'll see. I'd have to ask my parents. We may be going out of town. I'll call you back, okay?"

"Sure. Bye."

"Bye." Ibrahim hung up the telephone. He leaned back against his pillow to think.

⤸

That evening, Khalid was at his part-time job as a cashier at Super Foods, one of the grocery stores near his house. Usually he worked one or two evenings a week (less during soccer season) and on the weekends. However, because this was a short week of school, he was picking up some extra hours. The store was open on the morning of Thanksgiving and the Friday after as well. He had offered to work on both days, so he would get the extra holiday pay.

Whatever he earned went to his car insurance and gas, and anything left over he put into a savings account for college. He knew he wouldn't be able to save enough by the time he graduated in one-and-a-half years, but he hoped that with one year of full-time work after that, he would be able to start his studies. Any time he could pick up extra hours, he tried to take advantage of it.

All afternoon, the store had been especially busy, but now that it was later in the evening, things had slowed down. As he worked, Khalid thought back to the end of the school day when he had seen Ibrahim talking to a pretty blonde sophomore at his locker after school. She had appeared to be flirting with him and had touched his arm several times during their conversa-

MUSLIM TEENS IN PITFALLS AND PRANKS

tion. Khalid had meant to call his friend and make sure everything was okay. He worried about Ibrahim because he knew that sometimes his friend struggled to balance his religious beliefs with his desire to fit in and be popular at school. Khalid kicked himself for not taking the time to call Ibrahim before he came in for work.

A woman with a cart full of groceries came to his cash register, and Khalid busied himself ringing up her purchase. As she pushed her cart away, his supervisor approached with some change.

James was one of two supervisors at Super Foods, and he got along really well with Khalid. He was in his mid-forties and liked to discuss history and to learn about different languages. He was always asking Khalid how to say things in Arabic. Plus, he pronounced Khalid's name perfectly, unlike most people who called him Kaleed.

"Mr. Khalid, what's up? Are you making a lot of money for us tonight?" James greeted him.

"Of course. I only recommend the most expensive products," Khalid joked. He turned off his light.

"I know. That's why you're so good." James opened the cash register and began distributing the rolls of coins. "Actually I heard something really nice about you the other day. Frank Martin— he's one of our regular customers. Maybe you know him. He's a really nice older man, uses a cane. And he always comes to drink coffee in the deli. Poor guy. His wife has Alzheimer's, and he takes care of her at home. They've probably been married more than fifty years. Anyway, the day he was here, he said it was raining outside and even though we were so busy and you didn't have a bagger, you made him wait for a couple of minutes so you could finish with the people behind him and then you carried his groceries out and loaded them in his car for him. The next morning when he came here for breakfast, he told me all about it. He was just so happy."

"Wow, that was so nice of him." Khalid was genuinely surprised. He clearly remembered the incident. He silently reminded himself to thank Mr. Martin the next time he came in.

Just then, he noticed a group of four kids from his high school, walking past his register on their way into the store. Before he could even acknowledge them or say anything, one of them said, "Look, it's the Muslim terrorist."

"Hi, Saddam bin Laden," another one added as they all laughed. "Maybe we'll suicide bomb you."

Khalid had learned long ago to take these kinds of comments in stride and not to let them bother him. He knew they were just ignorant teenagers. James, however, was incensed.

"I'm sorry, what did you just say?" James demanded.

"Nothing," one of the boys smirked.

"Nothing? I don't think so. Tell me what you just said. Say it again. Come on."

"We didn't say anything," he lied again. "Who are you? Al Qaeda?"

By that time everyone was watching them. James was in his limelight. "You didn't say anything, huh? That's funny, because I heard you call this young man—*my employee*—a Muslim terrorist. I heard you call him Saddam bin Laden and then threaten him. Name calling is completely unacceptable and childish. And what's more, we don't allow anyone to threaten our employees. That's called intimidation, and it's a crime, a misdemeanor. Now get out of my store, and if I ever see any one of you in here again, I'll call the police."

The four teenagers silently filed out the doors, muttering to themselves. With that, several of the customers waiting in line began applauding.

James nonchalantly went back to filling the coin slots, and Khalid, slightly embarrassed from all of the attention, turned his light back on.

"I'll walk you to your car tonight," James told him as he walked away. "Just in case."

As Khalid continued to work, he thought about the incident. He thought the students were younger than him, probably sophomores. In general, he got along very well with everyone, especially since he was one of the best soccer players on his high school team and he was active in the student council. He was actually fairly popular, although he had experienced the occasional racist comment regarding his religion and country of origin. But, like most of the Muslim teenagers he knew, it was just something you had to put up with. He had never thought to react as angrily as James had that night.

The grocery store was open twenty-four hours, but Khalid always finished work at 9:00 PM or 10:00 PM. That night it was 10:00 PM. Just as he was clocking out in the break room, exactly as promised, James showed up to walk him to his car.

"I know I'm probably being overprotective," James admitted. "But I would expect the same thing from David's supervisor." David was his seventeen-year-old son. "And I would feel absolutely terrible if something happened to you."

"Nothing's gonna happen," Khalid assured him. "Those guys are long gone. Stuff like this, it happens. Just today, some kids at school did the same thing to my sister. You know, they just talk. They don't do anything."

"Well, it's still terrible. And your principal needs to do more about it. This isn't the 1960's anymore and racism is racism—whether it's directed against blacks or Hispanics or Muslims," James declared as they put on their coats. "I'm writing a letter to the editor about this. Or maybe I'll complain to the city council."

They slipped out the back door and into the employees' well-lit parking lot.

Generally, most of the other employees underwent a shift change at 11:00 PM, so Khalid usually left by himself. He had to admit, it was kind of nice to have some company for a change.

"So are you still trying to learn Arabic?" Khalid asked, changing the subject.

"*Na'am. Shway*," James laughed. "Aw, who am I kidding? Those are about the only two words I remember."

Khalid laughed, too, as they approached his car.

"Thanks a lot, James," he said gratefully. "Have a good night."

"You, too." Just as James turned to walk back inside, a car playing loud music suddenly screeched to a stop at the end of the parking lot. One of the people inside on the front passenger side threw something at them from his open window and then shouted, "Look at your new sign, terrorist lovers!" The car raced away.

James noted the license plate number, and he and Khalid looked up at the store sign. Just then, Khalid noticed that object that had been hurled at them was throwing sparks. It was a firecracker.

"James, watch out!" Khalid shouted, pushing his supervisor back as it suddenly exploded. He turned his face away and tried to shield James as well.

"Are you okay?" James demanded.

"Yeah. Just a little shook up. Are you?"

"Yeah. Look at the sign."

Khalid looked up again at the lighted sign for Super Foods. Painted in graffiti over the name were the words "Arab lovers" and "Home of the Terrorists."

"They will not get away with this," James vowed angrily. "Those are the same kids that were in the store before. I recognized one of the girls. She comes in here all the time with her mother. Well, she won't be coming here again."

"It's okay," Khalid said. "I'll come here early tomorrow morning before school, and we'll fix the sign."

"We will do no such thing. I'm calling the police tonight. And the newspaper."

"We don't want to make trouble or make things worse," Khalid protested.

"They're the ones making trouble. We could have been seriously hurt!"

"Well, *Alhamd-u-lillah*, we weren't."

"Yes, but I'm still calling the police. Go on home. I'll talk to them," James told him.

"Okay." Khalid unlocked the door and climbed into the driver's seat of his 1992 Toyota Corolla. He felt really drained, like he had worked more than just six hours. Plus, he was still kind of shook up. He started the car, still in a fog, and headed home.

When Khalid arrived at his house a few minutes later, his parents were still up. They usually waited up for him when he worked.

"How was work?" Mr. AlAmery asked in Arabic as Khalid slipped off his shoes and joined them in the family room. His mother muted the television. Although both of his parents spoke English, the family still always spoke in Arabic at home.

"Terrible," he declared. "These kids from high school made some really anti-Muslim comments to me while James was giving me some change. And he got really upset about it and kicked them out of the store. And then when I finished work, he walked me to my car, and the same teenagers drove past us and threw a firecracker at us." He went on to tell them what they had spray-painted over the sign and how the customers had applauded when James initially kicked out the troublemakers. Khalid smiled wryly. "They must have waited two hours in that parking lot for me. I wonder what they would have done if I didn't finish until midnight or 2:00 AM."

"I can't believe this." Mrs. AlAmery shook her head. "First Elham and now this."

"Well, I told him there's nothing we can do about it," Khalid said. "I mean, it's just the way people are. Luckily, stuff like this doesn't happen very often. I told James not to call the police."

"Well, he should have called the police," his father said emphatically. "This was wrong."

"I know, but what can you do? People are stupid."

"But it's different in America," Mr. AlAmery insisted. "Even if some people don't like Islam, we have freedom of religion here. That's why we came here—why the Hussains are here and other people."

"There's no freedom here," Khalid said bitterly. "They say there's freedom, but there isn't. You're only free in America if you look and act like everyone else. For anyone different—there's no freedom."

"Anyway, so what are they going to do about the sign and the other stuff?" Mrs. AlAmery interrupted. "Isn't it a crime to spray paint on the store sign and throw a firecracker?"

"I think so," Khalid sighed. "James called the police. At least he said he was going to. I left."

"Well, I hope that they find those teenagers and punish them," his father declared.

"James said he's going to call the newspaper, too. I told him not to. You know, I don't want to make this worse. But he said he didn't think it would. I don't know."

"I never expected people would be like that," his mother said, shaking her head. "Especially here in Iowa."

"But most people are okay," Khalid reminded her. "Like James. And all the people in the store. I was really embarrassed when that stuff happened, but now when I think about it, I feel so good that all of those people supported me like that. I mean, I didn't even know most of them, they were just customers."

"Yeah," Mr. AlAmery agreed. "That's really nice."

"Well, Khalid, why don't you go on upstairs and pray and get ready to sleep?" his mother suggested. "I think Farid's still awake, reading or something."

"Yeah, I am tired," he admitted. He headed up to the bedroom he shared with his younger brother.

Chapter 3

THANKSGIVING THURSDAY WAS AN ESPECIALLY busy day for the Karims. The day before, Mr. and Mrs. Karim had driven to Cedar Rapids to buy a halal turkey. They had started this tradition several years earlier when the halal grocery in Cedar Rapids first starting selling turkeys for Thanksgiving. Mrs. Karim had asked one of her American friends how to make stuffing, and now they enjoyed a traditional Thanksgiving dinner of roasted turkey, stuffing, salad, potatoes, and homemade bread.

Saad had invited two Saudi Arabian students from the university, and one of Mr. Karim's business partners and his wife were also going to join them. Mr. Karim worked at a local company as a mechanical engineer. Nur's friend Hafsa was also going to come.

That morning, Nur ambled into the kitchen, where Saad was talking to his mother. She was already busy cooking.

"So, anyway, Mom, I think they would be more comfortable if the men and women ate separately," Saad was saying.

"But that's not possible," Mrs. Karim protested. "We only have the dining room table."

"Can't you guys eat in the kitchen?" he pressed.

"At the counter?" she replied, glancing at the built-in kitchen table. "That's not comfortable. And besides, we only have four chairs here."

"Well, just bring an extra one for Mona." Mona was nine years old, the youngest Karim.

"What if we compromise? I'll seat all of the women and girls on one side, and you guys on the other," she suggested.

"I guess." Saad didn't sound very convinced.

"I mean, I don't understand. We have company all the time, and we always eat together," she continued. "Anyway, we'll see. What time are they coming?"

"I told them around noon."

"Well, I'll see what I can do."

"I can't believe you actually expect us to eat in the kitchen," Nur cut in angrily. "What are we—your servants?"

Saad glanced over at her. "You might want to learn some manners," he retorted.

"I have plenty of manners. Maybe if you were home more, you would realize that."

"Nur, grow up." Saad left the room to join his father and brother.

Nur picked up an apple from the bowl of fruit on the counter and began munching on it. "How come they wouldn't be comfortable if we ate in the same room?" she asked her mother.

Mrs. Karim shrugged. "Well, that's just how it is in some Muslim countries. Men and women eat separately and don't socialize together. It takes everyone a while to adjust."

"But I thought that was just when there's a lot of men and women together who aren't family, like on Eid," Nur said. "Or if there was just one woman and a few men."

"Well, it's not required with Islam. A lot of what people do is based more on traditions and culture than religion," her mother explained. "Like, take your father and brothers, for example. Your grandparents would be appalled if they knew that they all cooked sometimes and helped with other stuff around the house. And if they ever did that in Palestine, they'd talk about it for months. Because that is just the way they are traditionally. Traditionally, women do everything at home." Both Mr. and Mrs. Karim had grown up in the Palestinian territories.

"But I thought younger people were different."

"Well, remember that Saudi Arabia is a lot more conservative than some other countries. Anyway, we'll see. Listen, it's almost noon, so why don't you go change, and then come back and we'll finish the salad."

Nur wandered back to her bedroom to change her clothes. She hoped that Saad's friends were okay. She had met a few very conservative Muslims before and always felt somewhat awkward around them.

She threw on her nice black pants and a gray turtleneck sweater. Then she combed her shoulder-length hair and pulled it into a tight braid. Just as she was reaching for her green and gray hijab, Mona strolled into the bedroom.

"Can you braid my hair, too?" she asked.

"Sure." Nur put on her scarf and then brought the comb and a ponytail holder over to her bed. She sat down on the bed, and Mona sat on the floor below her.

"When can I start wearing hijab?" Mona asked as Nur combed her dark hair.

"Whenever you want," the older girl replied. "You don't have to until, well, for at least two or three more years probably. But you can wear it before that if you want. When I first met Elham, we were only ten, and she was already wearing hijab."

"Hmm… I don't know if I want to, though."

"Why not?"

"Because there's a couple of girls in my school now that do—like Asma, Hafsa's sister—but they say that people make fun of them a lot."

"Yeah, of course. Kids are stupid. But you still should wear it," Nur pointed out as she finished braiding Mona's hair.

Just then the doorbell rang. Nur stood up, checked herself in the mirror, and then she and Mona went downstairs. They had to walk through the family room to get to the kitchen, so they were able to see and greet Saad's friends from the university.

"*Salaam-u-alaikum,*" the two girls said together.

At their greeting, all of the men in the room stood up. "*Wa alaikum-a-salaam,*" they said in unison before sitting back down.

"These are my sisters," Saad said in Arabic. "Nur and Mona, this is Adnan and Yasser."

They exchanged hellos.

Nur and Mona joined their mother in the kitchen.

"Harmless enough, huh?" Mrs. Karim said with a smile.

"I guess," Nur shrugged.

"They even brought us flowers and a box of candy." Her mother nodded toward the gifts lying on the kitchen counter.

"Wow, can I have a piece?" Mona asked eagerly.

"Just one."

Before she could even open the box, the doorbell rang again.

"Oh, that's Hafsa," Nur said. "I'll get it." She hurried over to open the door, and found Hafsa and her ten-year-old sister, Asma.

"Can Asma come, too?" Hafsa asked. "She wants to see Mona."

"Sure, come on in."

Hafsa waved to her father in their minivan, and the three girls went inside the house.

"Mom, Hafsa's sister, Asma, came too," Nur said. "She's going to eat with us. Is that okay?"

"Of course, it's okay," Mrs. Karim said with a smile.

"Hi, Asma," Mona said happily. "Let's go play." The two younger girls skipped out of the kitchen and down the hall to Mona's room.

"Nur, can you take this juice into the family room and pass it around?" her mother requested as she finished pouring juice in glasses.

"Yeah, I guess." She reluctantly picked up the tray of glasses, carried it into the family room, and offered a glass to each of the men sitting there.

They were talking in Arabic about the plight of the Palestinians.

"The main problem in the Middle East is the occupation of Palestine," Yasser was saying.

"Of course, it is," Mr. Karim agreed. "But we have to be realistic. The occupation will never end, at least not anytime soon. We have to focus on our future. We need to find a way to end the violence and work on a peaceful solution."

"Yes! We need a solution," Yasser agreed. "But peace talks aren't the way. We have to show the Israelis we are strong. That we aren't afraid to die for our homeland. It worked in Lebanon, it seems to be working in Gaza, and I'm sure it'll work in the West Bank, too."

"But innocent people are getting hurt—Palestinians and Israelis," Mr. Karim argued. "Take my family. They live in Jenin. They are so tired from worrying about what is going to happen to them. Every time an Israeli soldier or settler is killed, they worry that their house is going to be destroyed. My younger sister just had a baby two months ago. A couple of settlers were injured in an attack a few days before she was due, and the Israeli soldiers shut down the entire city for three days, with curfews and checkpoints everywhere. She was so afraid that she would go into labor and not be able to get to the hospital. And those mortar attacks and suicide bombings… they kill innocent bystanders, women and children, people who never did anything wrong."

"Well, I have to agree with Yasser. Fighting for our rights is the only way," Adnan spoke up. "Of course, it's hard on the

people, especially the women and children. But it's the only way."
He shrugged. "The only way Palestine will be free."

"Maybe the people don't want to fight, maybe they just want peace," Nur said as she started to leave the room.

Adnan glanced briefly at her before turning back to Mr. Karim. Ignoring her remark completely, he said, "Believe me, making the Israelis suffer the way our people suffer, even if it causes a backlash of violence, makes the Palestinian people stronger. It is the only way we will win."

"Well, I don't agree. I think resorting to violence makes you weaker. It's wrong to kill people, whether they are Jews or Muslims or Christians, and—" Nur was interrupted by Saad's glaring stare. Shocked, she abruptly stopped talking, looked down at the ground and muttered, "Never mind." Embarrassed, she headed back into the kitchen. "Saad is such a jerk," she exploded, slamming the tray on the counter.

"What happened?" Mrs. Karim asked. She and Hafsa were sitting at the table, cutting vegetables for a salad.

"They were talking about peace and violence in Palestine, and I started to say something, but he looked at me so mean. I was so embarrassed. I just left." Nur joined them at the table and took the knife from Hafsa. She began hacking away at a cucumber.

"I'm sure he didn't mean anything by it," her mother said, trying to brush off the incident.

"Whatever. I'm not going to say anything to him until he apologizes," Nur declared.

Mrs. Karim smiled at Hafsa. "That may not really be a punishment for him," she said.

"Ha ha ha," Nur retorted. Inside, though, she was still seething. Was Saad embarrassed by her? What was the problem? She just wanted to give her opinion. Nothing wrong with that. Why was he acting so different? I will get to the bottom of all of this, she vowed silently.

Chapter 4

ELHAM LOOKED AGAIN AT THE OPINION page of Thursday's news-paper. "*Religious Bigotry Strikes Des Moines*" the headline read.

She still couldn't quite believe the events of the last few days had really happened. And she couldn't shake the bad feeling that the teens who had taunted Khalid at work were the same ones who had bothered her after school. It was so frustrating to know that they could get away with stuff like that. She was glad they had a few days off.

Elham let her eyes wander over the words one more time, still marveling that the editorial was so balanced and well-written.

RELIGIOUS BIGOTRY STRIKES IN DES MOINES

Late Tuesday night, the Super Foods on Bridge Street and two of its employees were the victims of a vicious hate crime. According to shoppers, four local teenagers entered the store early in the evening and insulted one of the cashiers, an adolescent of Middle Eastern origin. They went on to threaten him. The store manager heard the racist comments, and the threats, and responded by raising his voice in protest, asking the teens to leave.

The matter, however, didn't stop there. Later that night, as the two were leaving the store, the same teenagers allegedly threw a firecracker at the pair. It exploded just a few feet away from them, and, fortunately, neither suffered any

*serious injury. The teens also bragged of having spray paint-
ed the words "Arab Lovers" and "Home of the Terrorists" on
the store sign.*

*According to the American Islamic Organization (AIO),
a national Muslim organization dedicated to protecting
the civil rights of American Muslims, the number of hate
crimes against American Muslims continues to rise every
year. And, they are quick to add, these are just the reported
cases. There are many incidents that go unreported.*

*AIO also points out that Islamic organizations and cen-
ters nationwide, including the Des Moines Islamic Center,
have since 9-11 repeatedly denounced terrorism and violence against the West. Many, including our local mosque,
have taken pains to reach out to other religious organizations and groups to educate people about Islam and its
teachings.*

*We at the Des Moines Register find ourselves forced to
ask some hard questions. Have we carried stories about the
condemnations of terrorism and the outreach efforts of our
local Muslim community? Or have we focused only on violence overseas, contributing to the perception that Muslims
as a whole support such violence? Have we reported suffi-
ciently on the accomplishments—the bridges built—by in-
terfaith groups over the last few years, or have we reported
only what extremists have destroyed? We at the Des Moines
Register strongly denounce those who commit hate crimes,
and shudder to think that we may have in some way con-
tributed to the perception that such crimes are ever justifi-
able.*

Alongside the text was a picture of a charred circle on the pavement of the store parking lot, the defaced sign prominent in the background.

"That's a good editorial, huh?" Mrs. AlAmery asked as she joined her daughter in the dining room. Everyone else was in the family room, watching television.

"Yeah, it's okay," Elham agreed.

"Are you feeling a little better now?"

"Kind of. I don't know. I still don't want to go back to school, especially after what happened to Khalid."

"Well, don't worry about anything. I'm sure you'll feel better by Monday."

"I wish we had an Islamic school here like the one Zainab goes to in Minneapolis," Elham remarked. Zainab was one of her friends who used to live in Des Moines. She had moved to Minneapolis last year with her family.

"I know. I hate to see you like this. You're doing so good in school, and I know you like it a lot," her mother said.

"I like the classes, but it's not worth it," Elham replied. "I think I want to quit."

"Oh, Elham, of course, it's worth it. Look how far you've come. You don't want to quit now. You've been going to school here since first grade. You only have three-and-a-half more years left. Besides, you can't quit. I think that's against the law here."

"Yeah, but I hate it." Tears welled up in her eyes. "I want to move to Minneapolis and go to the Islamic school or I'm going to quit."

Mrs. AlAmery went over and sat next to her daughter. "Elham, you know you can't quit school. And you know we can't move to Minneapolis. Our home is here. All of your friends are here—Nur, Nadia, Hafsa. What would they do without you? I just talked to Rana, and she said she's been telling Nur for the last two weeks to work on her term paper. And she's just been struggling with it. And then you went over there for a couple of hours this Monday, and she said Nur was up until almost eleven o'clock because she was so excited to get part of it finished. What would she have done without you?"

"I'm sure she would have finished it. Or Nadia would have helped her."

"Not like you did." She paused. "Anyway, Ellie, we're not moving. Like I told you the other day, you can't just run away from your problems. Eventually, you'll find that there's no place for you to run anymore."

Just then they were interrupted by a loud thud against the front door. "What was that?" Elham exclaimed, jumping up.

"I'll get it," her father said firmly. He immediately went over to the door to see what had happened. Khalid and Farid were right behind him.

Mr. AlAmery gingerly opened the front door. On the other side of it was a large dent, right below the door handle. He looked down on the porch floor and saw a large rock with a paper attached to it.

"What is it, Dad?" Khalid asked. He and Farid peered around their father to see outside.

Carefully, with his foot, their father pushed the rock over to see the paper. Written on it were the words, "Go home, terrorists." There was no one outside in the street and no sign of suspicious cars.

"Oh, man," Farid gasped.

"I'm calling the police," Mr. AlAmery said soberly. "Don't touch or move that rock." He went back inside to get the telephone.

Within minutes a policeman had arrived. He talked mainly to Khalid about what had happened at the store the other night and then wanted to know if they had heard or seen anything suspicious that day. Wearing gloves, he put the rock in a plastic bag to take to the police station and look for fingerprints. Then he told them he was going to talk to some of their neighbors to see if anyone had seen anything suspicious, such as a strange or speeding car.

"You know," he added before he left. "I'm sorry there are people out there who do things like this. Back in the 1970's, when I was growing up in South Dakota, my neighbor and best friend was Sioux Indian, and I hated the way he was treated up in Sioux Falls because of it. I can't believe there are still people out there who can do things like this and think they can get away with it."

"Thank you," Mr. AlAmery said gratefully.

"Anyway," the police officer said. "I'll get this down to the station as soon as I talk to your neighbors. It's too bad this had to ruin your holiday."

"Thank you again." Mr. AlAmery closed the door after the police officer left.

By this point Elham was practically in tears. "I hate Des Moines," she sobbed. "I want to move."

"Elham, we're not moving and that's final," her mother said firmly. "Now, we need to finish making lunch. Idris and Sana will be here soon." Idris and Sana were both from southern Iraq and were close friends of the AlAmerys. Idris had lived in the United States for seven years. His wife Sana had just joined him four months ago. She was pregnant and due in the spring.

Before anyone could leave the room, they were interrupted by the ringing telephone.

Khalid picked it up. "Hello?" he said.

"Hello. Khalid?" the voice on the other end replied.

"Yes. James?"

"Yeah, it's me. Listen, I just wanted to make sure you all are okay. I knew you were getting off work at 11:00 AM this morning. Someone threw a rock on my front porch today with a note attached to it, nearly scared my family to death. And my parents are here for Thanksgiving. They're almost eighty years old, you know. Anyway, the police came and all. They think it was those same kids from the other night. They must have gotten my address from the phone book. Anyway, I just wanted to let you guys know, to watch out for something like that."

"Thanks, but I think you're a little late."

"Oh, no."

"Yeah," Khalid said soberly. "They did the same thing to us a few minutes ago."

James sighed loudly. "Well, that's terrible. Did you call the police?"

"Yeah, they just left."

"Well, listen, you guys hang in there. I know it's hard, but this will end, you know."

Khalid sighed, too. "We'll see. Anyway, have a happy Thanksgiving."

"Yeah, you, too."

Khalid hung up the telephone and turned back to his family. "That was James, my supervisor at work. He said that someone threw a rock on his porch a while ago. I guess, it had a note on it, too."

"Oh, no." Mrs. AlAmery shook her head in dismay.

"*Astagh-fir-Allah,*" her husband said under his breath.

Elham buried her head on her mother's shoulder in tears.

"Elham," Mr. AlAmery said sharply, "stop it."

Her mother stood up and put her arm around Elham, helping her to her feet. "Come on. Let's go in the kitchen."

They left the room just as the telephone rang again. Before anyone could even answer it, someone knocked on the door.

Mr. AlAmery and Farid went to answer the door, while Khalid picked up the telephone.

"Hello?" he said as his father and brother returned with Idris and Sana.

"Hello. *Salaam-u-alaikum*," Mrs. Karim greeted him.

"*Wa alaikum-a-salaam*," he replied.

"*Ummik mawjud?*"

"*Naam.*" Khalid took the receiver into the kitchen and handed it to his mother. "It's Mrs. Karim," he told her as Sana joined them.

She smiled at Khalid as he went back into the family room where his father, Idris, and Farid were discussing the events of the last few days, including what had just happened.

"Hello?" Mrs. AlAmery said into the telephone.

"Zahra, azizi, we heard about what happened," Mrs. Karim told her. "The police officer stopped at our house. Do you need anything? Is there anything we can do?"

"No, thank you. Thank you so much."

"No problem, of course. One of Ahmed's colleagues is here for lunch with his wife. And apparently when they came, as they turned onto our street, they were almost hit by a speeding car. They told the police officer about it, and he thought it might be the people who did this to you. He said the timing would have been right, and he was going to check into it. They gave him a description of the car but didn't know the license plate number," Mrs. Karim told her.

"Thank you, Rana. We really appreciate it."

"No problem," she repeated. "Do you want to come and eat with us?"

"No, thank you. Idris and Sana are here with us, so I already cooked." Mrs. AlAmery smiled at Sana.

"Well, you're all welcome, if you like. We always have room for more, although… you know, I just had a wonderful idea. Why don't you bring the food here and eat with us? Terry and Laura Kingsley, they're wonderful and they love Arabic food. And Saad has a couple of Saudi Arabian friends here from the university who don't really want us women eating with them, so we can all sit in the family room and relax. We'll let them have the dining room."

"Thank you so much, but I really don't think so."

"Please. Let Ahmed talk to Hassan. Just a minute."

Five minutes and a lot of bargaining later, Hassan AlAmery turned to his wife. "Will it be hard to take the food over there?" he asked.

She shook her head. "No."

Next he went back into the family room where their two guests were sitting on the couch. "Idris, Sana," he said in Arabic, "the Karims have invited us all to lunch with them. Is that okay?"

Idris looked at his wife, who nodded. "Whatever," he answered.

Sana laughed and patted her husband's stomach. "I think he means, as long as he eats, he doesn't care."

Mr. AlAmery smiled and then said back into the telephone. "Okay. Zahra says it's okay, and Idris and Sana just want to eat."

"Well, we have a lot of food," Mr. Karim assured him. "Come on over."

Chapter 5

Over an hour later, Mr. AlAmery sat back in his chair. "*Alhamdu-lillah*," he said with a sigh. "Thank you so much."

"You should eat more," Mr. Karim, as the host, encouraged.

"I can't," he insisted.

"Both of your wives are wonderful cooks," Terry Kingsley, Mr. Karim's colleague, complimented them.

"Thank you," the men said together.

"So what are you going to do now?" Yasser asked Mr. AlAmery. "Are you going to report this as a hate crime?"

"Well, I think we'll contact the American Islamic Organization. We don't really want to punish these teenagers, but they do need to be educated and maybe the AIO can help us and the mosque to do that."

"AIO?" Adnan sounded surprised. "I don't think they have that much power. I think it would be better to call the ACLU."

"They seem to have a lot of power. They have a lot of strong members," Mr. Karim argued.

"Yeah, they do," Yasser informed them. "But in the end, I don't know how much difference they really make."

"Well, at least they have contacts with a lot of other organizations like the ACLU," Mr. Karim said.

Adnan shrugged. "Well, then wouldn't it be better just to call the ACLU to begin with?"

"Well, maybe I'll talk to Musa or Yusuf," Mr. AlAmery said hesitantly. Musa Raheem and Yusuf Mahmood were the two imams at the local mosque, a Shia and Sunni respectively. He looked over at Mr. Karim. "Maybe if one of them calls the AIO, it'll be better."

⤺

Meanwhile, in the family room, all of the women had finished eating and had cleared the dishes away. Now Nur, Hafsa, and Elham were gathered around the kitchen sink, washing and drying the dishes while the water boiled for tea.

"You know, Ellie, everything'll be okay," Nur consoled her friend. "I mean, since we've known each other, this has happened a lot. I mean, remember last year during basketball? After almost every game people, even people from our school, would laugh at me and make fun of me. People are stupid. They do stupid things."

"I know, but not like this," Elham said. "I mean, I remember junior high, and how kids used to make fun of me, even when I was hanging out with Alexis or Maria or someone. But they never bothered my brother or my family."

"But, I'm sure if you ask Khalid, he'll tell you that kids have made fun of him before, too," Hafsa said gently. "It's just part of being a teenager in America. Anyone who isn't perfect, they make fun of, like the heavy kids or the special ed students."

"Imagine how Nadia's family felt during the war," Nur added. "People didn't just make fun of them or call them names. Muslims were actually tortured and killed just for being Muslim." Nadia had been born in Bosnia and had arrived in the US as a young girl seeking refuge with her family.

"I know," Elham admitted.

"And, you know, what Nur just said, she's not saying that what happened to you and your family is nothing. Of course, this isn't nothing. She just means you'll—we'll all—get through it," Hafsa explained.

"Yeah," Elham sighed. "I mean, with Nadia, she doesn't even remember the war, she says. And she says her dad never talks about it. I guess he was in one of those concentration camps. She says her mother was alone at home with them when that sniper hit her brother. Nadia was only two years old." Nadia had an older brother who had been killed by a sniper during the war in Bosnia. He was two years older than her.

"Yeah," Hafsa agreed. "Isn't it amazing what our parents have been through? My parents say they're lucky because they didn't have to leave Somalia until the end of the civil war, and we all left together, with us and my uncle's family. But we walked and walked, like, a hundred miles to the refugee camp in Kenya, and my mom was pregnant with Latifa at the time. And they say we're lucky because we were only in the camp two years before we came here. And all that was actually the fault of other Muslims."

"Yeah. That's what happened in Iraq, too." Elham sighed again. "I guess I'll be okay here."

"You will." Nur put her arm around her friend's shoulders. "I don't know what I would do without you." She was silent for a minute. "What is that noise?"

Hafsa giggled and turned off the stove. "The tea," she said.

"Oh." Nur took the box of loose tea and dumped a handful of black leaves into the tea kettle.

"Oh, man, Nur, what are you trying to do? That tea is going to be so black." Elham giggled, too. "I hope, for his sake, that you marry a chef."

"I didn't put in that much tea," Nur said defensively. "Besides, I don't like making tea. And just so you know, when I get married, I'm going to work, and my husband will stay at home and cook. So why do I need to learn how to?"

"You'll never find a man like that," Hafsa rebuked.

"Sure I will. I asked Saad about it one day, and he said he would love to stay home and let his wife work."

"Of course, he would," Elham replied. "Because men are lazy. But don't expect him to help his wife. They just want to lay around and watch tv. They'll still expect you to cook and do everything else."

"Well, then, I'll divorce him," Nur declared.

Hafsa and Elham laughed. "You make it sound so easy," Hafsa said.

"Anyway, I don't know why we're even talking about this," Nur said. "We're not going to get married for ages."

"Yeah," Elham agreed.

"I can't believe your dad's friend Idris is in our house," Nur said. "He is so cute. Did you see him, Hafsa?"

Hafsa nodded. "Yeah."

"He is cute," Elham agreed. "But he's taken. And besides, we're good Muslim girls."

"Of course, we are," Nur agreed. "But he's still cute."

Hafsa smiled. "Nur, you're weird."

Just then Mrs. Karim entered the kitchen. "Wow, Nur, the kitchen looks so nice," she complimented their work. "Thank you, girls. And you even made tea."

"Yeah. And maybe the next time we have a lot of company, we can use paper plates," Nur suggested.

Her mother laughed. "Nur, we're not going to use paper plates." She began pouring the tea into small glasses. "It sounds like your dad and those guys are finished, too, so if you just want to clear the table, I'll wash the dishes later." She finished pouring the tea, then put the glass sugar container on the tray, and whisked it all away into the family room.

"Sometimes I feel like a slave," Nur moaned.

"Nur, stop complaining," Elham reproached her. "I bet if you ask nicely, Saad and Ibrahim will help clear the table and wash the dishes."

As if on cue, the two boys appeared in the kitchen with a handful of plates. Mr. Karim and Khalid were right behind them with more.

"Since we washed all of the other dishes, can you guys wash yours?" Nur asked.

"No," Saad said disdainfully.

"We'll wash them," Ibrahim offered, to the surprise of the girls. "Right, Khalid?"

Khalid nodded. "Sure. Where's Farid?"

"I'm right here," his brother answered from somewhere behind them. "But I think I like Saad's answer better." He put the dishes he was carrying on the kitchen counter.

"It's okay. Khalid and I can do them. We'll be done in two minutes," Ibrahim informed him. He signaled at the girls to move, and then he and Khalid began rinsing the plates.

"What's going on here?" Saad's friend Adnan demanded as the rest of the men filed through the kitchen on their way to the family room.

Ibrahim turned around in surprise. "We're just helping out."

"This is women's work," Adnan protested. "Let the women do it. You should come visit with us. My father and brothers, they never do stuff like this. It's for women. It's a shame for you guys to do this."

Nur looked as if she was ready to explode.

Saad quickly intervened. "They just cleaned and washed everything. These guys are just finishing up. It's really nothing," he said, brushing off the boy's work.

"You girls have become too westernized, expecting men to help you with everything," Adnan admonished. "You should see the women in Saudi Arabia. They do twice as much as this every day and never complain. And if it's too hard for them, we get them a maid."

Nur could not control her temper any longer. "Why should I get a maid when I have two brothers?"

Saad shot her a you-need-to-calm-down look, but it was too late.

"Maybe if you asked your sisters, they would say they would *love* it if you helped them sometimes," she continued.

"Then I would bring them a maid. I told you, it's a shame for men to do this kind of work."

"Why would you pay someone when you could do the work yourself? That's a shame. Maybe that's why Saudi Arabia is the most backward country in the world for women!"

"Nur, that's enough," Saad said sharply. He nodded toward Adnan. "Let's go in there."

"You need to send your sister out of America for a while to study and get away from these westernized ideas," Adnan told Saad on their way out of the kitchen.

"Ooh, that makes me so mad!" Nur exploded. "Who is he to say that stuff?"

"Nur, no matter what, you still cannot behave like that with people. You need to be more respectful," Ibrahim scolded. "And you shouldn't talk about Saudi Arabia like that."

"He should be more respectful," she argued.

"No, he's older than you, and that's just the way he grew up. That's just the way it is where he grew up," her brother replied. "You're not going to change anything by shouting and making yourself upset. You need to be calm and rational."

"I am rational," she declared. "It just made me so mad the way he said that."

"You know, traditionally, that's how we are," Khalid spoke up quietly. "My family's the same way. I mean, Farid and I, we don't care. But my dad hardly ever cooks and cleans and stuff like that. And I'm sure if my aunts knew I was washing dishes while Elham was just standing right next to me, I'm sure they would go crazy."

"I don't know why," Nur said. "We all need to change."

"Anyway," Ibrahim said. "There's nothing we can do about it now. We're going to finish up here, no matter what Adnan says. And we'll make some more tea, so if you gals want to go somewhere, it's fine."

"That's okay," Nur said, sitting down in one of the chairs. "If we go to my room, we have to walk through the family room, and I don't want to do that. Maybe I'll get lectured about walking in front of men."

"Well, we can't just stay in here," Hafsa said, ignoring her comment. "It makes me feel guilty watching your brothers work while I just stand here."

"Don't feel guilty. This is more work than they've done all year," Nur said bitterly.

"Nur, do you want to wash the dishes?" Ibrahim asked.

"We can go to my house," Elham quickly intervened. "We'll have it all to ourselves, since everyone's here."

"Yeah," Nur agreed excitedly.

"Farid, can you go tell Mom to come here for a minute?" Elham requested.

"Why can't you?" he replied.

"I don't know..."

"I will when I take in the tea," Khalid offered as he began pouring tea into small glasses. After loading the sugar on his tray, he carried it into the family room.

A minute later, Mrs. AlAmery joined them in the kitchen, carrying a tray of empty tea glasses. "Did you need something, Elham?" she asked, setting the tray on the counter.

"Yeah. Can me, Nur, and Hafsa go over to our house to just hang out?" Elham asked.

"Yeah, that's fine." She smiled. "Let me get the key for you." She disappeared back into the family room.

Elham followed her but stayed right inside the entryway. Her eyes grew wide as she listened to part of the ongoing conversation.

Five minutes later, Mrs. AlAmery had handed her daughter the house key, and the three girls were walking across the street to Elham's house.

"How did Saad meet those guys?" Elham asked Nur.

"At the university. Why?" Nur replied.

"They seem so conservative," she said. "You know, while I was waiting for my mom to give me the keys, I heard them all talking. And those Saudi Arabian guys, they were still talking about women and stuff. And they were saying it's haram for women to wear pants." She shook her head. "Your dad was really arguing with them."

"Well, of course, it's not haram," Nur said. "As long as they're modest."

"My dad says that some people say it's wrong because in some Muslim countries, women don't usually wear them," Hafsa spoke up quietly.

"But it's not haram," Elham said quickly.

"No," Hafsa agreed.

"That really makes me mad," Nur said. "I mean, these people with their traditions, trying to say stuff is haram when it's not. They need to know what's really haram and halal in Islam, and not just say that something untraditional is haram. You know, in Islam, there's no hadiths or ayas that say men shouldn't help out at home. They all say men and women should help each other. And there's no hadiths that say women can't wear pants, so how do they know it's haram? There's no hadiths about smoking either, and they say that's okay. Even though it kills you. So what's wrong with pants?" she ranted. "Pants never killed anyone."

"I know," Elham sympathized as they approached her front door.

"Huh, they really hurt your door," Nur said, looking at the dent.

"Yeah." Elham shuddered. "Let's go inside. I hate being reminded of this."

They went inside the house. Hafsa closed and locked the door behind them. After removing their shoes, Elham went over to the phone to check the answering machine. There was one message.

"Hello, Mr. and Mrs. AlAmery," a man's voice spoke. "This is Sergeant Carter with the Des Moines police department. I just wanted to let you know that the description of the car seen in your neighborhood matched one owned by the family of one of the teenagers who was arrested two days ago, after the incident at Super Foods. When we questioned her today, she admitted to being the driver and gave us the names of the two other individuals involved. They've been arrested and put in juvenile detention until Monday morning when the courts reopen. Hope that makes you feel better. Happy Thanksgiving."

"Well, that's good," Nur said.

"Yeah, I don't know." Elham sat down on the couch. "But I just have this feeling that it's not going to end here. I mean… I don't know."

Hafsa sat down next to her friend. "Yeah, I know what you mean, but I'm sure it'll be okay." She tried to change the subject. "What's Nadia doing today?"

"Oh, she went out with her family," Nur answered. "I guess, there were a lot of Bosnian families getting together today 'cause of the holiday."

"Do you think I should call my parents and tell them about the message?" Elham asked.

"No," Nur said firmly. "You kept the message, so we're just going to forget about it for right now. Now, not to change the subject or anything, but I have a bigger mystery. What do you think about Saad? I mean, what's up with his friends? And now he's growing a beard. Do you think he's becoming an extremist?"

Hafsa laughed. "Growing a beard does not make you an extremist. Just like wearing hijab doesn't."

"And Saad's not like those guys," Elham added. "I mean, I don't think he agrees with what they were saying. He didn't seem to be arguing for them anyway."

"But he wasn't arguing against them either," Nur pointed out.

"Your brothers never argue. They're both so quiet and relaxed," Elham said. She looked over at her friend. "You could take some lessons from them."

"I'm quiet," Nur said defensively as Hafsa and Elham exchanged smiles. "What?" She lowered her tone of voice. "You don't think I'm quiet?"

"Well, you do talk a lot," Hafsa said truthfully.

"And you definitely like to argue," Elham added.

Nur pretended to pout. "You guys are mean," she said. "I don't like to argue."

Elham and Hafsa laughed.

"Huh," Elham said. "Let's see… what exactly did you say before? 'Why would you pay someone to wash dishes when you can do the work yourself?' Or it was something like that."

"I was making a point," Nur informed them, "not arguing."

"Ohhh, okay."

"Anyway, so you really don't think there's anything to worry about with Saad? The other thing I've noticed is that he speaks Arabic all the time now. I mean, usually we speak English at home except, you know, with guests and stuff like that. But lately he's always talking in Arabic. I mean, it seems like all of his friends are Arabic. He even talks to my parents in Arabic," Nur remarked.

"Well, I think you're worrying about nothing," Elham said with a yawn. "I talk to my parents in Arabic."

"I guess," Nur said, but she didn't sound very convinced.

Meanwhile back at the Karims, Ibrahim and Khalid were finishing up the dishes and straightening the kitchen. Farid had wandered into the family room and was listening to the adults' conversation.

"Hey, Khalid, do you have a sec?" Ibrahim asked as he hung up his dish towel.

"Yeah, what's up?"

"Well, you know, there's this girl at school. She's a sophomore. Her name's Christy," he began.

"Yeah, I saw you talking to her the other day. What about her?"

Ibrahim sat down at the kitchen counter. "Well, she asked me to go to this party tomorrow night." He paused. "Do you think it would be okay to go?"

Khalid joined him at the table. "Oh, man… well, I don't know. I mean, I think you have to expect that the people there will be drinking and stuff, even doing drugs," he told him. "I mean, I know those kids seem really cool and good and stuff, but… well, like back at the beginning of school, Brian and I went to this party after one of our soccer games, and we got there a little late. Half the kids were drunk already and making out and stuff. We just left right away." Brian Lentz was a fellow soccer player.

"That's sick." Ibrahim sounded disgusted.

"You just have to kind of pick and choose," Khalid continued. "I mean, some of the guys on the soccer team, like Brian or Mark, they're pretty clean. We've gone out before, and they don't drink or anything like that. They just go to school and work and study really hard."

"Yeah."

"Anyway, if you want my advice, don't even bother going. I mean, it's not worth it. You'll just feel pressured and then guilty, and why put yourself in that situation?" He paused. "Why don't you hang out with me tomorrow night? We'll get some movies or something."

"Okay, but, Khalid… do you ever, like, want to date?"

"Yeah," he nodded. "I do sometimes. I mean, it seems so cool to have a girlfriend and all. But, you know, you have to stay with Islam. It's the only way."

"So what makes you so strong?" Ibrahim asked.

"I guess I just don't want to feel guilty," Khalid said, "because I know I would if I put myself in that situation or did something haram. I felt guilty just going to that party, without even doing anything there."

"Yeah, I don't know how people can be like that. I mean, these are the same people who are drinking and all on Saturday night and then go to church the next day like good little teenagers. How can you—I mean, why do you think it's like that? I don't know. I mean, sometimes I just think how nice it would be to fit in and be like everyone else," Ibrahim continued.

"Yeah, I know what you mean," Khalid agreed. "But you have to think that there's twelve hundred students at our high school. And these people are, I don't know, not even ten percent of them. So ninety percent are just like you. And besides, would you really want to go out with a girl who's already had probably ten other boyfriends?"

"Yeah." Ibrahim sighed.

Khalid looked over at his friend. "You know what, man? Just go to the party. I mean, see for yourself. I trust you. I know you won't do anything wrong. I'll back you up."

"That's okay. I don't need to see for myself. I know you're right."

"Maybe it'll make you feel more sure."

"No, that's okay." Ibrahim sighed again. "I know that dating is wrong. And I know that I would feel bad if I did go to the party. So you're right. We'll just hang out together tomorrow night."

Chapter 6

THE NEXT MORNING, NUR ATE an early breakfast with her parents and Saad. She liked waking early on the weekends or school holidays, so she could be with her parents and have them all to herself. Neither of her parents were working that day, but Saad had to be at the bookstore by 8:30 AM. Everyone else was still asleep.

Nur, still in her sweatpants and t-shirt, dug in hungrily to her bowl of cereal. "So do you agree with what your Wahabi friends were saying last night about women?" Nur asked her brother.

"They're not Wahabi," he informed her.

She rolled her eyes. "Whatever. Do you agree with them?"

"Well, kind of." He shrugged.

"I knew it." She waved her spoon at him. "You're becoming a crazy extremist."

He looked at her as if she were crazy. "I am not becoming an extremist," he said.

"Yes, you are. You're growing a beard. You're speaking Arabic all the time. You've got those crazy Wahabi friends. You probably want us all to wear burqas, don't you?"

"Nur!" her mother reprimanded.

"They're not Wahabi," Saad repeated. "And you're nuts." He poured himself another bowl of cereal and added milk to it.

"I am not!"

"A lot of Muslim men have a beard, like Imam Mahmood, and Mr. Hussain. And a lot of people speak Arabic all the time, like your little friend Elham. And for the fifteenth time, those guys are not Wahabi. They're just two nice boys from Saudi Arabia who happened to be alone for the holidays. Do you think the AlAmerys would have been comfortable with them here if they were Wahabi? No! Because Wahabi people hate Shias! Now stop acting so crazy."

"Sor-ry." Nur looked down at her bowl. "So what did you mean when you said you kind of agree with them?"

"I mean, I kind of do. When a man works and a woman doesn't, she should take care of the house," he said. "It's only fair. And I don't really want my wife to work, except maybe part-time."

"You don't hate Shias, do you?"

"No!" he practically shouted. "And neither do Adnan or Yasser, which I've told you a million times if you would just listen. They're just very traditional. They're not married yet, and neither one of them has been here very long. A lot of the stuff here in the U.S. is still really new for them."

"Well, I hope they get married soon and bring their wives here. Then I'll teach them some things about women's rights and being a feminist," Nur said.

"That's great. I'll be sure to warn them well ahead of time. Don't bring your wife around Nur or you'll have to make your own dinner tonight," Saad said sarcastically.

Nur smiled. "That's right."

Mr. Karim yawned. "My goodness, I thought you kids stopped being so noisy a long time ago," he remarked. "So what have we learned? Is Saad an extremist now? Or is growing a beard okay?"

"Daddy, be serious. Aren't you worried that your oldest son is hanging out with those Wahabis?"

"For the fiftieth time, they are not Wahabi!" Saad exclaimed.

"Okay, Saudi Arabian. Whatever. Aren't you worried 'cause he's hanging out with them? What if he becomes Waha—Sau— too conservative and extremist? I mean, pants are not haram!"

Saad took his empty bowl over to the sink. He started to wash it, but then turned the water off and left it alone. He turned back to his younger sister. "You know, I was going to wash my bowl, but you're just being a little too annoying today, so I think I'll leave it for you. Oh, no, what did I just say? I'm asking my sister—a woman—to wash my dishes! I hope I'm not becoming Wahabi." He started to leave the room.

"Saad, you're a jerk. And I'm not washing your stupid bowl!" Nur called after him. "I'll leave it until you get home from work and you can wash it yourself."

"I'll wash it," Mrs. Karim offered.

"Mother!" Nur exclaimed.

"What? I don't mind."

Nur poured herself another bowl of cereal. "You should mind. You're not his slave," she reprimanded.

"But I don't mind. Saad's going to be working hard today, plus studying. You guys wash my dishes when I work," her mother pointed out. "It's all about compromise. I have to wash the dishes anyway. Don't go to the other extreme, Nur. Men and women will only get along if they work together and compromise."

"What if they push Saad to become like them?" Nur asked quietly.

"Actually they were both very nice," Mr. Karim spoke up. "I was with them the whole afternoon, and they were very nice. Traditional, but not too conservative. They talked to Hassan—Elham's father—about Shias and seemed to appreciate what he told them. And they even wanted to see our mosque after they heard how it is."

"Hmmm… anyway, we'll see."

About an hour later, Saad was long gone to the bookstore. Ibrahim had just woken up and was in the shower. It was the perfect time to nose around in their room a little to see what Saad had been reading lately. Or so Nur thought.

She slipped into her brothers' bedroom, leaving the door open to ensure that she could still hear the shower running. Then she wandered over to Saad's bookshelf. She skimmed over the book titles and, not finding anything unusual, quickly glanced at the books on the small shelf above their desk. Most of them were textbooks and binders. However, one caught her eye. It was called, *The Roots of Arab Nationalism.* "What's nationalism?" she asked herself.

Just then she realized that the shower was no longer running. "Uh-oh, I wonder how long it's been off," Nur thought frantically. However, before she could go anywhere, she noticed an overseas telephone number and e-mail address written on one of the papers on the desk. It said OL followed by the number. She tried to memorize the phone number as she hurried out of the room.

Less than five minutes later, she was on the phone with Elham.

"Nur, it's nine o'clock in the morning on a holiday," Elham complained after her father had called her to the telephone.

"Sorry." Nur didn't sound apologetic at all. "But we need to talk."

"About what?"

"Saad."

Elham groaned. "Oh, not again."

Nur ignored her comment. "Listen, I was in his room this morning—"

"Snooping?" her friend interrupted.

"No," Nur said testily. "I was just looking around. And anyway, I found this book called something about Arab nationalism. Do you know what that means?"

"Nationalism? I don't know."

"Huh. You're supposed to be smart."

"Thanks. Why don't you ask Ibrahim or your dad? I'm sure your dad knows what it means." Elham paused. "Can I go back to sleep now?"

"No, I have something else to tell you. I found the initials OL and a foreign phone number written on one of his papers. It was 011966, and I don't remember the rest. But the country code 966 is for Saudi Arabia. I looked it up."

"Well, I don't know. Do you have any relatives in Saudi Arabia?"

"No. And I don't know anyone whose initials are OL either," Nur replied.

Elham groaned. "Well, I don't know. I'm tired. Maybe it's Osama bin Laden. Isn't he from Saudi Arabia?"

"Oh, no. Oh, no! Do you think so?"

"No, Nur. I was just kidding."

"Well, that would make sense."

"It does not make sense," Elham interrupted. "It doesn't at all. I was just kidding. There are a million other names that start with O. Like Omar and Othman, and tons of others. Now, forget what I just said. I was just kidding. Let's talk about something else."

"There's nothing else to talk about," Nur said dejectedly. "My brother's becoming a terrorist."

"Nur Karim, don't you ever say that again!" Elham exclaimed. Suddenly she sounded more awake than she had during their entire telephone conversation. "Your brother is a very nice boy, and he is not a terrorist. And if you ever say that again, I'll tell your parents! Now, I'll tell you who OL is. It's the family of one of his Saudi Arabian friends. That's who it is. One of the ones who was at your house last night. And that makes a lot more sense to me."

"You're right! I knew they were Wahabi. I'm sure OL is Osama bin Laden, and he's related to them. I heard that some of bin Laden's relatives live here in the US. Oh, what are we going to do?" Nur wailed.

"We are not going to do anything," Elham said sharply. "You are going to stop making false accusations against those two guys. Just because they're a little conservative doesn't mean they're Wahabi. My dad said they were very nice and, you know, Wahabis hate us. And you know what it's like when people call you names and accuse you of stuff."

"I know."

"So put this one out of your mind," Elham continued. "OL is not Osama bin Laden. It's just some nice man or woman who happens to live in Saudi Arabia."

"Huh. Do you think it's a woman?"

"I don't know. Maybe they're trying to find a wife for Saad," she suggested.

"Huh," Nur said again.

"Anyway, can I go back to sleep now?"

"How can you still be asleep?" Nur demanded. "It's 9:30."

"Yeah, it's too early. I stayed up late last night. Maybe you can go back and wander around Saad's room a little more."

"I can't. Ibrahim's in there now."

"Just a minute," Elham said. Then Nur heard her saying, "What? No, it's Nur. Okay. Just a minute. I'm not done yet." She returned to the phone. "Nur, Farid needs to tell Ibrahim something. Probably I'll call you later. I'm going to the mosque with my parents for Friday prayer if you want to come."

"I'll see. Call me before."

"Okay. Bye."

"Bye. I'll get Ibrahim." Nur took the phone into Ibrahim's room. "It's Farid. He wants to talk to you," she told him.

Nur wandered back into her bedroom and lay down on the bed to think. Mona was out using the computer, so she had the bedroom to herself.

She knew that she sometimes jumped to conclusions that later turned out to be wrong. Was it really possible that Saad could change so drastically? And what if OL *was* a Saudi Arabian woman, one he might even be serious about? Actually, that's what she should hope for at this point, because the alternative was that her brother was turning into a terrorist.

Chapter 7

ANYTIME SHE COULD, ELHAM LIKED to go to the mosque for the Friday prayer. She enjoyed the large gathering of local Muslims, the readings of the Quran, and the speech that followed the prayer. This Friday, her father was going to make an announcement afterwards that he wanted to organize a group of Muslims to go and talk to the junior high and high school principals about the harassment of Muslim students and what could be done to help with this problem.

He had thought of this yesterday evening, after everything that had happened to his family that week. He had talked to Imam Raheem, the local Shia imam, who was very supportive of the idea.

Khalid was working, so it was just Elham and her parents, plus Farid. However, Nur was coming with her family, and Nadia would be there with her father as well.

The Islamic Center of Des Moines was unique compared to other mosques across the country. Because there wasn't a large Muslim population in Des Moines, either Sunni or Shia, leaders from the two sects felt it would be more practical and economical to have one center for both groups. They had combined resources and bought an old house that had been renovated into apartments. On the main floor, in each of the apartments, they had torn down walls, making one big room. Upstairs, each imam had a bedroom for his office. In the hallway between the apartments, they had put in large built-in shoe racks. This way both sects of Muslims could pray in separate areas but still socialize together in the center.

All of this came about when Sunni leaders at the mosque had noticed that occasionally Shias would come once or twice to pray but then wouldn't return and would not participate in some of the other mosque activities such as Eid al-Fitr. After reaching out to the Shia leaders in the community, they all came up with this solution. Each large room was separated down the center with a folding curtain, so the men and women could pray separately, yet the women could still hear the khutbah. And later they added curtains in the back so when you entered the praying area, you could proceed from the back to either enter the area for men or for women without interrupting.

The two bedroom apartment in the basement had also been transformed. Each bedroom had been turned into a classroom, one for women and girls, and the other for men and boys. The former family room was used as a library with some chairs, couches, and tables. There were also several bookshelves along the walls lined with books on Islam, Islamic and Middle Eastern history, and Arabic.

Although the mosque did not have a daily school, they did offer weekend classes for children eleven and up. These were classes on the Quran and religion (one each for girls and boys). They also offered English classes and tutoring for newcomers to the United States. Because the center was a joint Sunni-Shia effort, they discouraged specific sectarian education inside; rather, the imams encouraged their followers to pursue this at home. All of the classes were designed for both groups together.

All of the members of the Des Moines Islamic community were very proud of their center and the sense of community it provided. Although heated discussions and arguments did occur occasionally, all of the members considered themselves friends and knew that in a country where they were still considered to belong to a "foreign" religion, they had to work together. Once Imam Musa Raheem, a devout Iranian Shia, was asked to give a speech for a Shia mosque that had just opened in a mid-western city a few hours away. When he spoke about the sense of community between the Sunnis and Shias in Des Moines, many of the crowd were very surprised. Afterward, they told him that, although they did have a separate center, they were going to visit the Sunni mosque and reach out to their community more.

Usually after Friday prayer, all of the Muslims gathered in the Sunni area to hear the imam's speech. The two imams generally alternated weeks. According to their bylaws, they could not discuss controversial issues, but rather were to use this time to speak about issues agreed upon by all Muslims such as the Quran and its teachings.

After the prayer, Imam Raheem talked about the story of Yusuf, as told in the Quran. Then it was Mr. AlAmery's turn to talk.

Elham was so proud of her father. In general, he was fairly reserved and did not like speaking in front of large groups of people, especially in English. However, this was an issue which had deeply touched him in the last week, and he felt he could not stay silent. It also helped that he knew almost everyone who attended the mosque, Sunni and Shia.

"As usual, before we leave, it's time for any announcements," Imam Raheem said. "And today, as far as I know, we only have one from Hassan AlAmery. If there are any others, please follow Hassan."

Mr. AlAmery stood up and turned to face the small crowd. "This week, some really sad things have happened here in town to me and my family, and it has made me realize how much work we still have to do to get rid of Islam's negative public image." He paused. "One thing I've realized is that our kids, especially our teenagers, put up with way too much abuse and ridiculing at school. I would like to organize a group of concerned parents to talk to the principals of our local junior high and high schools, so they can perhaps be more aware of the problem and more willing to do something about it."

"I absolutely agree," Khalil Azizi, a Pakistani-American, spoke up. "My kids aren't even in school yet, but I know how the high schools are here. I would be very interested in helping out."

"Having grown up here and gone to school at North Des Moines High School, I know what it's like to be made fun of because of religion and to not have anyone to help you," his wife, Shireen, added. "I remember denying my religion because I didn't want to be teased. I absolutely do not want other kids to have to go through what I did, if we can do something about it."

"We left Bosnia because we were persecuted for being Muslim," another man said. "Now my kids are picked on in school because they are Muslim. I don't want them to have to deny their religion, too."

Several others spoke up in agreement, and in the end fifteen people expressed interest in working with the AlAmerys. They decided to divide up into five groups to visit the two high schools and the three junior high schools where the majority of Muslims attended. They agreed to try to set up times to meet with the principals for the following week.

As the AlAmerys left the mosque that day, Hassan let out a deep sigh of relief. "That went a lot better than I expected," he said.

"Yeah, everyone was so nice," his wife agreed.

They were interrupted by Nur's voice. "Elham!" she called, hurrying to catch them before they reached their car. Nadia was with her.

Elham turned around expectantly. "What?"

"I need to talk to you about, you know, what we talked about this morning. Do you want to come over? Nadia's coming."

Elham looked over at her parents.

"It's fine," Mr. AlAmery assured her. "It just means one less kid we have to worry about for lunch."

Elham rolled her eyes as she joined her friends.

"Be home before dark," her mother warned.

"So what did you want to tell me?" Elham asked curiously.

"Just wait until we get home," Nur said secretively. "Because we have to ride with my parents."

Fifteen minutes later, the three girls had just settled down on Nur's bedroom floor. However, before anyone could say anything, the bedroom door opened and Mona walked in.

"I want to hang out with you guys, too," she whined.

"Later, Mona," Nur told her brusquely. "We need to discuss something in private and then you can hang out with us."

"I can keep a secret. And besides, it's my room, too."

"Later, Mona," Nur repeated impatiently. "Go talk to Ibrahim."

"He's in his bedroom."

"Well, go help Mom with lunch."

"Daddy's helping her."

"Well, I'm sure there's something she needs. And you can come back in, like, half an hour and hang out with us, okay?"

"Twenty minutes?" Mona said hopefully.

"All right, twenty minutes. Just go!"

Mona smiled triumphantly and looked over at the alarm clock—1:34 PM. Then she slipped back out the bedroom door.

Nur closed the door behind her and turned back to her friends. "All right, we have to be fast," she said. "I already told Nadia everything about yesterday, you know, with Saad's friends. And I told her about the phone number I found. But I didn't tell you guys what else I found."

"Did you ever ask your dad about the word nationalism?" Elham interrupted.

"Yeah, and he said it was when you think your country is the best. He said Arab nationalism is thinking Arabic people are the best," Nur replied.

"Huh."

"Anyway. So I went back to Saad's room later, and I found this in his jeans drawer." She dramatically reached under her pillow and pulled out a piece of paper with the words Hamas, intifada 2, and Al Qaeda in Iraq written on it.

"This was just laying in his jeans drawer?" Nadia asked doubtfully.

"No, it was in one of his pockets," Nur replied.

"You went through his pockets?" Elham exclaimed.

"I had to!" Nur said defensively. "And you would not believe what I found in there. Money, nail clippers, his driver's license, tons of papers…"

"His driver's license? So how does he drive without it?" Nadia wanted to know.

"I don't know. He probably forgot it was in there. Anyway, what do you think of this paper?"

"What about it?" Elham asked.

"Don't you see? I think Saad wants to go to fight," Nur told them. "I should have known this would happen. I mean… I just don't get it. Why Saad?"

"Well, I don't think this really means anything," Nadia said, not sounding very sure.

"It does if you put everything together… like how he's changing and like his friends who just happen to be related to Osama bin Laden…the phone number and e-mail address in Saudi Arabia… and now this."

"Well, we don't know if those guys are related to Osama bin Laden. I still think OL means someone else," Elham consoled her. "And maybe he was going to ask someone else about Hamas and stuff."

"So what about the book about Arab nationalism?"

"I don't know, but I'm sure there's an explanation for all of this if you just ask Saad," Nadia said rationally.

"I don't think so," Nur said despondently.

"Well, you can't keep snooping around his room," Elham snapped. "You need to find out what's going on."

"Well, I can't just ask him."

"Anyway," Elham said. "Enough. Let's talk about something else. I'm so nervous about going back to school on Monday."

"Yeah, I know," Nadia said sympathetically.

"I hope nothing else happens."

"Nothing will happen, Elham." Nur sounded impatient.

"Nur, you're not the only one with problems," Elham snapped.

"I know that. But… I'm only talking about Saad so much to take your mind off everything else."

Elham could not help laughing. "Yeah, right. But I guess you're right. I shouldn't think that much about it. So what time will Saad be home?"

"I think he finishes around 5:00 PM," Nur replied.

"So we still have time to snoop around a little more," Elham said impetuously.

Nadia groaned. "Oh, no, Elham. Not you, too."

"The problem is Ibrahim. As long as he's home, he just stays in his room," Nur said.

"Oh, that's not a problem. We'll send him over to hang out with Farid. Plus, I think Khalid'll be home around 3:00 PM," Elham suggested. "And, besides, all I really want to do is look inside that book and see if anything's highlighted. And I think you should ask your parents if they've noticed anything different about Saad."

"Great idea. You're so smart," Nur said. "We'll talk to them at lunch, and we'll get Ibrahim to leave right after we eat."

Just then the bedroom door opened, and Mona entered. She joined them on the floor as Nur glanced at the clock. It was 1:54 PM exactly. Leave it to Mona to not be a single second late, Nur thought to herself.

"What are you guys doing?" Mona asked.

"Just hanging out," Nur said shortly. "Do you know what they're making for lunch?"

"Kabob and bread. I think a salad. I think hummus. I heard Mom say she doesn't want to have a big dinner tonight, so we'll have a big lunch."

"Wow, your mom's kabob is so good," Nadia said.

"I know how to make kabob," Nur boasted.

"Really? So maybe you can show me how. I want to make it for my family."

"Sure. Sometime when my mom's working, I'll make it and you can watch," she suggested.

"I don't know how you and your family are all so thin," Elham said. "The way your parents cook. I love your dad's baklava." While Mr. Karim was in college in the West Bank, he had worked at a Palestinian bakery. He still occasionally baked desserts some twenty-five years later.

"I like the kunafa. Once we got kunafa from this Palestinian restaurant in Minneapolis, and your dad's is so much better," Nadia said. "He should open a bakery."

"Yeah, he should," Elham agreed. "I would stop there every day for baklava."

"So this is what you guys do? Just talk about food?" Mona said disdainfully.

"So what did you expect?" Nur demanded.

"I don't know. Gossip."

"We don't gossip," Nur informed her. "It's not nice, and plus, it's wrong."

Just then they heard Mrs. Karim call them to lunch.

Mona stood up. "Thank goodness," she said with relief. "You guys are boring. After lunch I'm just going to read."

The other girls stood up, too. They put their hijabs back on and followed her out of the room.

Chapter 8

THAT DAY FOR LUNCH, THE KARIMS had spread out a tablecloth on the family room floor to eat. Sometimes they still liked to eat on the floor. Elham's family almost always sat on the floor for meals, but the Hussains usually ate at the table.

"This kabob is so good," Nadia complimented. "How do you make it?"

"It's actually really easy," Mrs. Karim told her. "I just dice up an onion really small and mix it with the ground beef. And I add a little flour or rice flour and then salt and pepper. And then I just broil it in the oven and put the sumac on top."

"Wow, it does sound easy," Nadia said.

"It is. Remember, I told you I'd show you how to make it? Later," Nur said impatiently. She paused. "So, Mom and Dad… you haven't noticed anything different with Saad?"

"Like what?" Mr. Karim wanted to know. "Are you still obsessed with the idea that he's becoming too extremist?"

"I'm not obsessed," she denied. "I'm just worried about him."

"Well, don't be," her father instructed. "Based on what you were talking about this morning—the beard and the fact that he's speaking Arabic more—you have no grounds to worry."

"What about his friends?" she persisted. "The two Saudi Arabian guys?"

"Nur, Saudi Arabia is a big country and most of its people, like most Americans, are good people. It's just the government that's corrupt and conservative," he lectured. "And besides, as we've told you again and again, those young men are very traditional. They're not basing their arguments on religion, on Islam. They're basing them on Saudi traditions."

"Okay, I have another piece of evidence," she said.

Mrs. Karim smiled at her daughter's choice of words. "What is that?"

"Well, the other day I found him reading this book about Arab nationalism," she announced dramatically. She hadn't really found him reading it, but he must have at some point or he wouldn't have it, right?

"So that's why you were asking about nationalism," Mr. Karim said. "Interesting. Well, that's good. I'm glad he's interested in politics." He took another bite.

Nur felt ready to explode. How could her parents be so complacent? "You're glad?" she exclaimed. "How can you say that?"

"Nur Karim," her mother said. "You want to be a lawyer, right? And a lawyer argues cases, but she has to have proof to argue. With all of these small points that you bring up, you don't have any proof, and that's why we're not concerned."

"Well, what if one of those guys from Saudi Arabia is related to Osama bin Laden?" she demanded, putting down her spoon.

"Is he?"

"Maybe."

"Maybe because you have proof or maybe because he's from Saudi Arabia and Osama bin Laden's from Saudi Arabia, so there's like a 0.00001% chance?" Mr. Karim replied.

"Well, I might have proof," she hedged.

"What proof?"

"Never mind, just forget it. Ask Saad. I don't want to talk about it anymore." Nur started eating again.

"That's fine with me," Mr. Karim declared.

"So when can you show me how to make kabob?" Nadia asked her friend, trying to change the subject.

"My mom already told you how," Nur said grouchily.

Nadia was taken aback by Nur's gruff reply. Mrs. Karim smiled sympathetically at her.

"So, Dad, you really think that Saad's okay?" Nur persisted.

"Yes, Nur, for the tenth time. Maybe you see him changing a little, but there's nothing wrong with change," her father replied.

"I guess." Nur didn't sound very certain. "I will find out what's going on," she vowed to herself. "I will get to the bottom of this."

⤸

After lunch, Ibrahim wandered back to his bedroom for a few minutes. He could not stop thinking about Christy.

I wish I could go to the party tonight with her, he said to himself, forgetting all memories of the conversation he had just had with Khalid the day before. Immediately he felt guilty for his thoughts. I just need to stop thinking about it. Maybe I'll call her and that will help. Actually, maybe I'll call Mark.

Mark Wilson was a fellow sophomore who played soccer with him. Although Ibrahim knew that Mark would have a difference of opinion with the advice that Khalid had given him, deep inside he kind of wanted that.

Ibrahim stood up and headed back out to the family room where his parents were washing the dishes. "Mom, Dad, I'm going to use your phone, okay?" he requested.

"Why can't you use the one in the family room?" his father replied.

"Because Nur and those guys are all in there. There's too much noise." Afraid that his parents thought he was being too secretive, he quickly added, "I'll use it in your room if you want."

"Yeah, that's fine," Mr. Karim agreed.

Ibrahim went back to his parents' bedroom and quickly dialed his friend Mark's phone number.

"Hey, Ibrahim. What's up?" Mark greeted him.

"Not much. What's going on there?"

"Nothing. I'm just sitting at home with my parents. My grandparents are visiting us from Missouri."

"Oh, well, I won't keep you," Ibrahim said quickly. "I just need your opinion."

"Sure. What's up?"

"Well, you know Christy Duncan, the cheerleader?"

"Yeah, she's pretty hot. What about her?" Mark replied.

"She asked me out," Ibrahim informed him. "Actually she asked me to go to some party tonight, but she said she also wants to go out with me."

Nur happened to be walking past her parents' bedroom when she heard Ibrahim's voice. Wide-eyed in surprise and curiosity, she paused to listen more.

"Well, I don't know about the party. There'll probably be a lot of drinking and stuff," Mark said. "But you can still go out with her. That's pretty cool actually. Will you remember me when you're cool and popular?"

"Yeah, of course. You're one of my best friends. So you think it'd be okay to go out with her on Monday or Tuesday? Like on a date?"

"Sure. Where would you take her?"

"I don't know. Somewhere quiet where there's not a lot of people around from school, where we could talk," Ibrahim answered.

"Sounds nice. I bet with someone like her, you'll be able to do a lot more than just talk. Let me know how things go."

"What do you mean, a lot more than just talk?" Ibrahim asked.

Nur's mouth dropped open in shock. Just then she realized that her brother was getting ready to hang up. She hurried back out to the family room where her friends were waiting for her. This was huge! Ibrahim, her brother, was going out with a girl. She could definitely use this information to get whatever she wanted from him. But she had to keep it a secret, even from her best friends. "What's going on with my family?" she asked herself. "First Saad, now Ibrahim. Boy, am I going to have some fun."

⤺

Friday morning had been really slow at the grocery store. Khalid had expected it to be busy, since it was supposedly the biggest shopping day of the year. But, I guess, he thought, not too many people are buying groceries. Even into the early afternoon, it remained slow, though a steady flow of customers trickled in.

The sign for Super Foods had been removed two days earlier, and they were going to erect a new sign next week. Khalid was glad it was gone. He didn't want any reminders of the terrible events before Thanksgiving.

That day, Khalid had alternated between working at the cash register and unpacking and stocking. He tried very hard to familiarize himself with everything in the store because when he was stocking, it seemed like people always asked him where stuff was.

As he was stacking cans of vegetables on the shelves, James stopped by. He had not worked yesterday, so this was the first time he had seen Khalid since Tuesday night.

"Hello, Mr. Khalid," he greeted him. "How's it going?"

"Great," he replied. "How was your Thanksgiving?"

"It was good except when those stupid kids threw the rock on my porch. That scared everyone in my family, especially my parents. Boy, am I glad they caught them."

"Yeah," Khalid agreed. "What'll you think will happen to them?"

"Oh, nothing, of course," James said nonchalantly. "They'll probably release them from juvenile detention on Monday, and then they'll go to court and probably have to pay for our new sign and your door. And maybe they'll be fined. But that's about it." The nice thing about James was that he was very up front and honest. He never tried to hide anything and would tell you things exactly how they were.

"Well, anyway, it doesn't matter," Khalid said. He continued shelving the cans of vegetables.

"Of course, it matters," James said vehemently. "Kids need to learn a lesson. They should be punished. Kids these days get away with way too much."

"Yeah. My dad and some other Muslims from the mosque are going to talk to the high school and junior high principals this week about everything, especially all of the harassment at school," Khalid told him,

"Well, good for them! That's exactly what they need to do. It's amazing how ignorant teachers and principals are to all the bullying that goes on in school."

"I think they try to ignore it."

"I wouldn't be surprised. Did you read the editorial in the newspaper?"

"Yeah, I thought it was okay."

"Yeah. You know, my parents still live in Martin, the little town I grew up in. And my dad—he's just the typical gruff Iowa farmer. Anyway, after he read the article yesterday, he said to me, 'If anyone bothers these Muslims again, you tell them they need to answer to me. My doctor's from Pakistan. He's Muslim, and he's the best darn doctor I've ever had.' And then he said he would never trade his doctor for another silly Christian boy. Isn't that crazy?" James said with a laugh.

"Yeah, that's really nice."

⤴

Meanwhile, back at the Karims, lunch was finished and the kitchen was clean. Ibrahim had gone over to the AlAmerys' house, Mr. and Mrs. Karim were using the computer, and Mona was in the bedroom reading. The coast was clear to begin the search.

Nadia and Elham had decided that Nadia would stay behind and keep an eye on Mona while the other two girls explored. This way, she could also alert them in case Ibrahim returned unexpectedly or her parents came down the hall.

"Remember," Nur whispered to her friend as they stood in the hallway outside the boys' bedroom. "If anyone comes, tell them we're looking for a CD. Got it?"

"Yeah, yeah, I know," Elham said impatiently. "Anyway, let's go."

"Wait a minute. Remember, when you look in the book, you're looking for anything highlighted or marked, underlined, stuff like that. Anything related to terrorism."

"All right. I know. Now, let's go."

"Relax. We have plenty of time. Okay, let's go."

The two girls entered the bedroom, and Nur closed the door partway. "That book is over there, on the shelf above the desk." She nodded toward the desk. "I'm going to look in his backpack."

"I feel kind of guilty," Elham admitted. "I don't think we should be in here after all."

"Don't be crazy. Now, go!" Nur gave her a little push.

Elham reluctantly went over to the small shelf over the desk. She looked through the book titles and found the one on Arab nationalism. Then she pulled it off the shelf and began skimming through it.

"The whole book is highlighted," she complained quietly.

"Well, keep looking at it," Nur whispered back. "See what's highlighted. Anything about terrorism?"

Elham paged through the book more slowly. "I don't know," she said. She turned back to the table of contents and found the list of chapters. "Actually, I think the whole book's about terrorism," she griped.

"Man, I don't even know my brother anymore," Nur said. "I can't believe some of the stuff he has in here." She pulled out a small case of CDs, opened it, and found a couple of contemporary and classical CDs as well as one of recitation of the Quran. There was also one of teachings from Al Azhar University in Egypt, but the CD inside was missing. She glanced at the cover which was completely in Arabic.

"There's nothing in this book," Elham concluded. She put it back on the shelf. "Where else do you want me to look?"

"What do you mean there's nothing in the book? It's so thick. Did you even look at it?" Nur demanded quietly.

"Yes, I did," Elham snapped.

"All right, well, I don't know. Look under the bed, maybe."

Elham moved toward the bed. "I feel like a criminal."

Just then they heard Nadia's voice from next door. She seemed to be talking rather loudly.

"I doubt if your book is in Ibrahim's room. Why would he have a Nancy Drew book? Besides, Elham and Nur went out to the kitchen, so let's just hang out, you and me," she was saying.

"Yikes!" Nur said softly. She began throwing everything back into Saad's knapsack. Elham seemed frozen in place.

Mona said something, but her voice was muffled.

"I'll help you find your book later. Let me do your hair," Nadia's voice was loud and clear.

Elham giggled. "I didn't know Nadia could talk so loud."

"Shhh," Nur hushed her.

After a few seconds, they heard Nadia say, "You know, you have such nice hair."

Nur sighed with relief. "Okay, we need to hurry. Look everywhere. Just hurry!"

Those words only succeeded in making Elham more frazzled than she already was. To Nur's annoyance, she actually began to straighten the desk.

"Elham!" Nur snapped. "What are you doing?"

"What?"

"Don't clean! Look in the drawers and stuff. Come on, hurry!"

Elham opened the bottom desk drawer and found a bag of Snickers. "Oh, wow. Want a Snickers?"

"No, I don't want a Snickers!" Nur snapped. She was looking under Saad's bed, but quickly stood up. "Come on, let's go."

The two girls started to leave the room, but Nur paused by the door. She quickly turned around, went back to the desk, opened the bottom drawer, and took out the bag of candy bars.

"Trust me, they'll never know," Nur said defensively as they left the room. She quietly closed the door behind them. "They'll just think they finished it." Nur opened her bedroom door, and she and Elham entered the room.

They found Nadia sitting on Mona's bed with Mona on the floor below her. Nadia was brushing and styling Mona's hair. Nur threw the bag of candy on the bed.

"Where'd you get the candy?" Mona demanded.

"We found it in Saad and Ibrahim's desk. We were looking for something."

"Wow. I'll be right back," Mona told Nadia. She crawled over to the edge of the bed and grabbed the bag of candy before returning to her previous seat. She passed small candy bars around the room. "Thanks, Nur."

"Did you find what you were looking for?" Nadia asked slyly.

"No," Nur said dejectedly.

"You know, it's so fun hanging out with you guys," Mona said, happily eating her candy bar while Nadia brushed her hair. "We should go search their room more often. I bet they've got tons of food hidden in there."

"I don't know, but what if you bring us some water or juice or something?" Nur suggested.

"Do you want me to make juice?" Mona offered. She turned to the other two girls. "I make really good fresh juice, and we still have tons of fruit from yesterday."

"Yeah, that would be great!" Elham said, sounding a bit too excited.

Mona did not catch her tone of voice. She jumped up off the floor, sending the hairbrush flying across the room. "Sorry," she apologized to Nadia, running to retrieve it. After putting it back on the dresser, she hurried down the hall to the kitchen.

"Man, she has just a little too much energy," Elham commented.

"Just like Lena," Nadia agreed. "Just running all over the place. I don't remember being like that when I was eight."

"I'm sure we weren't," Nur assured her. "Anyway, we didn't find anything."

"Well, don't be disappointed," Nadia consoled her. "Actually, you should be glad."

"I guess," Nur said.

"Maybe it's not as bad as you think," Elham tried to comfort her. "I mean, maybe if you just talk to him a little or get your parents to talk to him a little, maybe he'll change back like he was before."

"Maybe." Nur didn't sound very convinced.

Chapter 9

MONDAY MORNING AT THE KARIMS, all of the kids were getting ready to go back to school after their Thanksgiving break. Mrs. Karim had left for work already, and Saad had an early class so it was just Mr. Karim and the other three at the breakfast table.

"Dad, I might hang out with some friends after school for a while," Ibrahim said, trying to sound casual.

"With who?" his father demanded.

"With Mark, you know, from the soccer team. You've met him before."

"Oh, Mark. The blond guy. Doesn't he have a girlfriend now?" Nur asked.

Ibrahim glared at his sister. "No," he said emphatically.

"Well, I thought I saw him with a girl the other day," Nur continued.

"It was probably his sister," her older brother replied.

"No, it wasn't his sister."

"Does he have a girlfriend?" Mr. Karim interrupted.

"No, he's too busy studying. He's one of the smartest guys in our class." Ibrahim knew that mentioning that would win him some points. In his father's mind, hard-working students didn't have time for girls and parties.

"Oh," Nur said suddenly. "I was confused. Mark's the one with the long hair."

"It's not long," her brother informed her.

"Well, it is kind of," she said innocently.

"Nur…"

"You know, I would kind of like to meet Mark again before you just hang out with him. Is anyone else going to be with you?" their father spoke up.

"Yeah, Hamid." Ibrahim knew that would score points with his father also. Hamid Mukhtar was another friend, a senior who did well in school and worked and was very similar to Khalid. He often gave them rides to and from school.

"So who's going to drive me home?" Nur demanded, temporarily forgetting her charade.

"You can ride with Elham or Nadia," her brother snapped. He turned back to Mr. Karim. "So is it okay, Dad?"

"Yeah, as long as you're home by dark. What are you going to do?"

"Since the weather's supposed to be okay, we're going to the park to play some basketball or something," Ibrahim lied.

"Really? Well, maybe I'll come with you and walk," Nur suggested.

Ibrahim glared at her again. Why was she being such a jerk? "You're not invited," he said simply.

"Alright, alright, just be home by dark." Mr. Karim pushed back his chair. "Okay, you guys, go finish getting ready. It's almost time to go."

The kids quickly put their dishes in the dishwasher and scattered to prepare for the school day. Nur smiled to herself. There was nothing like having the upper hand with her brothers.

﹏

At the same time, a nervous Elham sat in the front seat of Khalid's old Toyota Corolla as he drove her and Hafsa to their high school. None of them really talked that much on the way, and when Khalid parked the car in the school parking lot, Elham let out a dramatic sigh.

"I guess, I have to go in, huh?" she said, only half-joking. A part of her hoped Khalid would say no, they could skip school that day. But no such luck.

"Yes, Ellie, it'll be fine. Come on, everyone's waiting for us," he told her.

Elham closed her eyes and sighed again. "*Bismallah rahman-i-raheem,*" she said to herself, and then opened her eyes and climbed out of the car.

"You walk in front, I'll walk behind her," Khalid told Hafsa, "to make sure she doesn't make a run for it."

"I don't feel good," Elham complained as they walked toward the school building.

Khalid ignored her. "You weren't at the mosque on Saturday, were you?" he asked Hafsa.

"No. My mom was working, so I had to watch my sisters," she replied.

"Is Fatemeh still trying to pray?" Fatemeh was Hafsa's four-year-old sister.

Hafsa laughed. "She thinks she is, but she's not. She just copies what I do and says *Allah-hu-akbar.*"

Even Elham had to smile. "That's so cute," she said.

"Yeah," Hafsa agreed. "At least she's really quiet and doesn't try to interrupt."

As they approached the front doors and were surrounded by more and more other students, Elham suddenly stopped walking. "Khalid? I can't do it," she said quietly, almost in tears. "I can't go inside."

"Elham, come on," he pleaded. "Believe me, it'll be fine."

She started crying. "I can't," she sobbed. "Please don't make me."

Hafsa put her arm around her friend. "Elham, you have to," she said quietly. "Believe me, you're a lot stronger than you think. And Allah's watching out for you."

"But what if something else happens?"

"If it does, it does. It's not up to us. It's up to Allah," Hafsa told her. "And you can't spend your whole life in hiding."

Elham wiped away her tears. "Okay."

"Listen," Khalid said seriously. "We're all going to be together before class, and I will come to your locker as soon as school is finished. Then we'll go to mine together before we leave."

"And since we have lunch at the same time, I'll meet you at your locker before lunch," Hafsa added.

"Promise?"

They both nodded solemnly.

The three students entered the building and quickly located their friends. Elham and Hafsa found Nur and Nadia with a couple of other Bosnian girls. For the five minutes before the bell rang for first period, Elham was able to relax a little with her friends, although she could not help checking around her for the kids who had taunted her last week.

When the bell finally rang, she walked to her science class with her friend Alexis. Although she had always liked science, she hated the class this year because of her teacher. The only good thing about it was that it was first period, so she finished it right away. Her second period was world history which she really enjoyed. Third was geometry (not her favorite) and fourth period she had English, another class she really liked. Then she had lunch followed in the afternoon with art, Spanish, and health.

Before lunch, just as promised, Hafsa met her at her locker. She had Kate, another sophomore, with her. And after school, Khalid was waiting for her at her locker when she got there. He really was a good brother.

"How was it today?" he asked.

"Fine." She sighed with relief. "Much better than I expected," she admitted, opening her locker. "I think I'll be okay tomorrow." She exchanged some of her books and then closed the door.

"I'm sure you will."

"I have tons of homework tonight, in almost every class," Elham declared as they walked to her brother's locker, where Hafsa was waiting patiently for them.

"Yeah, the teachers do that a lot after a holiday," he agreed.

Ten minutes later, the three teenagers were in Khalid's car as he backed out of his parking space. Elham felt much more like her normal self than she had that morning. She was sitting in the front, next to her brother.

Among his friends, Khalid was well-known for his crazy driving. His father said he drove like a "typical Iraqi." He was the only one of the AlAmery, Karim, and Hussain kids to have his driver's license, so they often joked that they were stuck with him. That day was no exception.

They had left school a little late, so there wasn't as much traffic in the parking lot as usual. The high school was on a small side street that led to one of the main streets in the city. As Khalid pulled out onto the busy road, Elham shrieked, "Khalid, did you not see that car?"

"It was ten miles away," he retorted.

"No, it wasn't. It's right behind us."

"Relax," he said. "Yikes." The traffic light ahead of him had changed from green to yellow, and he braked quickly to avoid hitting the car in front of him.

Elham turned around to face her friend. "You know, a couple of weeks ago we were driving downtown, and we were on A Street, looking for this bookstore. And we just passed it and didn't realize it, so Khalid—for real—backed up on the street to park in front of the store. I thought for sure we were going to die or at least get arrested."

Hafsa laughed as the car screeched forward. Elham turned back around.

"It was raining," her brother said defensively. "I was making it easier for you. I could have parked where we were, but I didn't want you to get wet."

"Didn't want me to get wet or you?" Elham scoffed.

"Oh, come on." He looked over at her. "I'm a nice guy."

"Khalid, I hate it when you look at other people while you're driving," Elham rebuked. "You should be looking at the road."

Khalid glanced at the road and then turned back to his sister. "Should I be?" he teased. "It seems like you're looking at it enough for both of us."

"Khalid!" she exclaimed. "Don't be a jerk!"

Khalid looked ahead at the road and sighed. "You're right. I don't want anything to happen to Hafsa." He glanced at her in the rearview mirror and smiled.

"Ha, ha, very funny."

He stopped at another red light and looked over at his sister. "It's so nice to see you in a better mood," he commented, affectionately patting her on the head.

She pushed his hand away. "Well, I feel better. Actually school was okay. Even Mrs. Falls was okay."

"Good. I didn't have her, but I've heard pretty bad things about her."

"Oh, yeah, she's so prejudiced," Elham said. "No one likes her, except the popular kids."

"It's green," Hafsa spoke up from the back seat.

Khalid looked at the traffic light. "Thanks," he said as he began driving again.

"She treats all of the international students terrible," Elham continued. "Actually all of the non-popular students. I can't wait to finish her class."

"Well, I think she teaches some chemistry classes, too, but just pay attention to the teachers when you sign up for those."

"Um, Khalid, you missed our street," Hafsa informed him.

"Oh, I did?" He braked abruptly so he could turn on the next street.

Elham's head jerked back and then fell forward, and she grabbed the back of her neck. "Ouch!"

"Sorry." He affectionately patted her head again. "You okay?"

"Fine," she grumbled.

Khalid swung around back to the street they needed. They passed the small street where the mosque was and the street that Nadia and her family lived on before turning left on Hafsa's street and pulling up in front of her apartment building.

"See you tomorrow morning," she said as she climbed out of the backseat.

"Bye! Thanks for everything today, Hafsa," Elham called after her.

"You're welcome," Hafsa replied. "Have a good night."

As usual, Khalid waited until she had safely entered the building before starting to drive again.

"Thanks for everything today, Khalid," Elham said sincerely. "I really appreciate it. I mean, I really do."

Khalid smiled at her. "No problem. I know it was a hard day for you. But, look, the day's finished, and tomorrow will be easier. Trust me."

"I hope so. But I'm a little worried that if those kids get out of jail or whatever today, maybe they'll try to make problems tomorrow," she fretted.

"I don't think so. They'll be on probation, so if anything else happens they know their punishment will be much stronger. And I'm sure it'll be okay," he assured her. "We'll just do the same thing we did today."

"Oh, man, Khalid, what's wrong with you today? You just missed our street!" Elham exclaimed.

"No, I didn't. Are you serious?" He looked in the rearview mirror. "Huh." Because it was a quiet street and there were no cars, he u-turned at the next intersection. "Anyway, like I was saying, it'll be just like today. No problem."

"Thanks," she said gratefully as he pulled into their driveway. "Wow, I'm glad you didn't drive past our house."

Khalid reached over and patted her on the head again. "You're so cute," he teased.

"Be quiet," she retorted as they climbed out of the car and headed inside the house.

Chapter 10

As Khalid and Elham were leaving the high school, Ibrahim was standing by his locker when he heard a familiar girl's voice behind him, just as he had hoped and expected. He was glad he had planned ahead by telling his parents he was going to hang out with his friends after school.

"Hey, Ibrahim." Christy leaned against the locker next to his.

"Hey, Christy," he replied casually.

"So, do you want to go out with me today?" she asked coyly.

"Well… like where?"

She smiled and twirled a wisp of her blonde hair. "We could walk over to Farley Park. It's pretty nice outside."

"Hmm." Ibrahim thought for a minute. Even though that was a big park, sometimes he and his friends played soccer there, plus it wasn't very far from his house. It seemed kind of risky. He might be seen. "Well, if you want to walk we could go to the Drake campus," he suggested. "It's not that far, and it's pretty nice." Drake University was a large college near downtown Des Moines.

"Okay, let me just tell my brother, so he can pick us up. Maybe he'll drop us off, too." She grabbed his hand. "Come on."

Ibrahim pulled his hand away and finished getting his books. Then he followed her down the hall to the seniors' locker area. They approached a tall, blond-haired boy who Ibrahim didn't recognize.

"Greg, can you drop me and my friend off at Drake?" Christy asked. "We want to walk a little."

Her brother turned around. He saw Ibrahim and held out his hand. "Greg," he said simply.

"Ibrahim," Ibrahim introduced himself, shaking his hand.

"Oh, yeah, you're on the soccer team, aren't you?"

"Yeah."

Greg turned back to his sister. "Sure, I'll drop you. What time do you want me to pick you up?"

"Maybe 5:00 PM or 5:30 PM," Ibrahim suggested.

"Sure."

The three teenagers headed out to the parking lot and over to Greg's green Jeep Cherokee. It looked almost new, a far cry from Khalid's old Toyota Corolla. Ibrahim sat in the front and during the ride, he and Greg kept up a steady conversation about school and sports. Greg was a varsity basketball player, but he seemed to follow all of the school sports. Since Saad had just graduated a year ago and had been one of the top soccer players, he even remembered Ibrahim's older brother and asked what he was doing now. He seemed really surprised that Saad was still living at home and commuting to college and working.

Ten minutes later, Greg pulled up in front of one of the main buildings on the Drake University campus.

"So, I'll pick you up here at 5:00 PM," Greg said as they climbed out of the car. "Don't be late."

"Okay." Christy rolled her eyes.

Her brother drove away, and the young couple started walking.

"Sorry about him," she apologized. "He's a little overprotective."

"That's okay," Ibrahim reassured her, but inside he was thinking, Overprotective? This is overprotective? He just dropped me off here with his little sister, and he doesn't know anything about me. I went through the third degree this morning with my dad, and I told him I was just going out with friends, not even a girl.

"So," she said as they walked along one of the paths. "I'm glad you went out with me. You seem really shy."

"Yeah, I don't really date," Ibrahim said honestly.

"Oh, I don't believe that. I mean, you're so cute. Plus, you're such a good soccer player. You've probably got girls falling all over you. I thought maybe you already had a girlfriend and maybe that's why you didn't want to go out with me."

"Well, no, I don't."

Christy reached over and started holding his hand. "So, maybe I can be your girlfriend."

Ibrahim felt a little uncomfortable, but he tried not to show it, and he didn't take his hand away. "Maybe," he said.

"Let's sit down for a minute," she suggested as they approached a bench.

They sat down and were quiet for a few seconds before Christy suddenly leaned forward toward him and kissed him on the cheek. Ibrahim was taken by surprise and pulled back.

"What's the matter? You don't like me?" She pretended to pout.

"No, I do." He leaned against the back of the bench.

Christy leaned in toward him again, but Ibrahim quickly cut her off. He stood back up. "Christy, we don't even know each other," he said.

"What's to know?" She shrugged. "I like you, and you like me. That's enough. Or, at least, I thought you liked me."

"I do," he assured her. "But I just don't want to move too fast."

"We're just kissing."

"I know. Come on. Let's walk a little." He signaled for her to stand up.

She reluctantly relented and stood back up. "Okay. So where are you from?" she asked as they began walking again.

"What do you mean?"

"I mean, aren't you from a different country?"

"No. I was born here, probably at the same hospital you were born at."

"Wow, I don't know which hospital I was born at," Christy said. "But my birthday's February 24."

"Mine's April 7," he told her.

"Huh, so I'm almost two months older than you." She paused. "But if you were born here, how come you have a different name?"

"Ibrahim?" he said. "It's Muslim. It's just like Abraham."

"So you're Muslim? Like those terrorists?"

"Muslims aren't terrorists," he corrected her. "Some terrorists are Muslim, just like some are Christian."

"Sor-ry!"

"It's okay. People say that all the time."

"I guess I don't know that much about Muslims," she admitted. "Except from TV."

"Well, I can teach you," he said.

"Maybe later. Right now, the only Muslim I want to know more about is you."

They continued to walk and talk (and flirt), and Ibrahim couldn't believe it when five o'clock came. In the beginning he had felt really nervous and guilty about being with her. But actually it was fun, and he had had a really good time. It felt kind of nice to be walking with a girl, talking and being together. Several times, she had tried to hold his hand or give him a kiss, and each time Ibrahim pulled away. Even so, in the end, Christy had asked him to call her.

As Greg drove them home later that afternoon, he hoped that no one would see them pull up. Luckily it was almost dark, so no one should be outside. He was kind of embarrassed by their house and middle class neighborhood. During the walk, he had learned that Christy's father was a dentist, which explained her brother's nice car. But she seemed genuinely impressed when Ibrahim told her how his father had come here and worked his way through graduate school and now worked as an engineer.

"Our house is here, on the left. You can just stop here," he instructed.

Greg pulled over opposite their house, and Ibrahim climbed out of the jeep. "Thanks a lot," he said, taking his backpack off the floor.

"No problem."

"Call me," Christy said. "I'll see you tomorrow."

"Bye." Ibrahim closed the door and headed over to his house. He made it inside without anyone suspecting a thing. After calling out greetings, he hurried upstairs to his room.

"Hey, what's up?" Saad greeted him. He was sitting at the desk working on homework.

"Nothing. What's up with you?" Ibrahim threw his backpack on the floor and sat down in the other chair.

"Just doing some calculus."

"Can you take a break for, like, fifteen minutes?" the younger boy asked. "I need advice."

"Yeah, sure. What's up?"

"This girl wants to go out with me," Ibrahim blurted out.

"Oh, wow. Non-Muslim, right?" Saad asked.

Ibrahim shrugged his shoulders. "Yeah, of course."

"Well, I think you know the answer."

"But I really want to go out with her."

"Why?"

"I don't know. She's really cool and popular. She's a cheer-leader. I know I could control myself. It's not really wrong unless you do something, right?"

"Well, if you do go out with her, she's going to expect you to do something," Saad told him. "Because at some point she's going to want to hold your hand or expect you to kiss her. This is why dating is wrong. Not because it's wrong to talk to a girl. Of course, that's not haram. Just being alone with a girl isn't wrong if both of you can control yourselves. But Allah knows that isn't possible. At some point one of you is going to touch the other one. And maybe hug and kiss and you know…"

"But girls and boys hug on TV, and they're just friends," Ibrahim argued.

"That's TV."

"Anyway, what if we just go out once or twice? I'm sure nothing will happen."

Saad shrugged. "Well, it's up to you."

"Didn't you ever want to have a girlfriend?" Ibrahim persisted.

"Of course," his brother replied. "But you have to control yourself. You can't always have what you want. And if you can't control yourself, get married."

"I'm too young to get married," Ibrahim grumbled.

"Well, then you're too young to date."

"Why can't I just have fun?"

"Well, Ibrahim, it's up to you. If you think it's okay, then fine. Go out with her."

"Other Muslim men, they date. Like, Jawad," he pointed out. "And he's an adult."

"You're right, Ibrahim. He does it, so of course it's okay," Saad said. "Anyway, I need to do my calculus." He turned around and faced the desk.

"Saad, don't be mad. I mean, I know it's wrong. Believe me, I know it's wrong. But… I don't know…"

Saad turned back around. "I'm not mad," he said. "I mean, I trust you. You know, ultimately it's up to you. No one's going to blame you if you give in and date this girl. I mean, that's the easy thing to do. Just like what you said with Jawad. But the hard thing is to do what's right."

"Yeah."

"And besides," Saad continued. "Anything wrong for women is wrong for men. Do you think that Jawad would let his sister date? Would you let Nur?"

"That's different," Ibrahim started to say.

"No, it's not. If it's okay for you, it should be okay for her, too," he argued.

"I see your point," Ibrahim agreed. "So if I go out with her, will you be mad?"

"Of course not," Saad assured him. "Ibrahim, it's up to you. It's really between you and Allah. Just be careful. I mean, don't do anything you're going to regret."

"Like what?"

"Like… anything."

"Anyway," the younger boy said, changing the subject. "I've got some homework to do, too. I need to finish it."

As Ibrahim turned back to his math and began working through some problems, he couldn't stop thinking about Christy and the important decision he had to make. He wanted to do the right thing, but he also really wanted to be cool and accepted by the popular crowd at school. "Surely going out with her a couple of more times would be okay," he rationalized. "We won't do anything. And then I'll be cool and I won't need her anymore. So I'm actually not going out with her to date, just so I can be popular. So it would be no big deal, right?"

Suddenly, he realized that he had missed his prayers for Zhuhr and Asr. He glanced over at Saad, who was still hunched over the desk, hard at work.

"Oh," Ibrahim said to himself. "If I pray now, I'll have to explain to Saad why I missed them. I'll just make them up tomorrow."

Chapter 11

THAT EVENING, ELHAM HAD GOTTEN permission from her parents to do her homework over at Nur's house. Now, she and Nadia were sitting on Nur's bedroom floor finishing up while Nur sat on her bed. All three had books spread out around them.

Suddenly Nur set down her book and papers. "My term paper is officially finished," she announced. "I'm going to type it all tomorrow night and turn it in on Wednesday."

"Super," Elham congratulated.

"It is super, isn't it?" Nur said proudly. "I have to turn it in by next Monday, and I'm actually going to turn it in early. Can you believe that? Me, Nur Karim, is turning homework in early!"

"Speaking of homework, I think my geometry is done," Nadia said. "Thank goodness. I hate math. Just give me one example as a hair stylist when I'm ever going to use geometry."

"What if someone asks you, what's the area of my hair?" Elham challenged.

"I'll tell them to go ask Mrs. Winsler," Nadia replied, "because I don't answer geometry questions."

"Funny," Elham said sarcastically. "I'm so tired. I had homework in science, geometry, Spanish, and history. Just English I didn't have homework in, and I have that stupid term paper due Monday in that class."

"I thought you finished it," Nur said.

Elham sighed. "I did. And it's almost all typed. I just hate typing."

"How was science today?" Nur asked.

"It was okay," Elham replied. "It's not bad for me every day. But every day Mrs. Falls picks on someone."

"It must be terrible," Nadia said sympathetically.

"It is. I hate it. All the kids in my class are popular, except," she paused to count, "just a few of us. And we're the only ones that Mrs. Falls picks on. Today it was Maria's turn."

"What happened?" Nur wanted to know.

"Well, she was really tired because she helps out at her parents' store, and she was working last night. And we have science early. It's first period. Anyway, Maria was so tired, she couldn't really pay attention especially when Mrs. Falls asked her questions. So then she made her stand up and read out loud for, like, ten minutes," Elham told them.

Nadia shook her head in disbelief. "You guys should complain about her," she said. "Ali has her, and he tells me the same stories."

"Ibrahim said some students did complain last year, and it didn't do any good," Nur said.

"Well, maybe if people keep complaining they'll eventually fire her," Nadia replied.

"Well, I told Mr. Kinzey what she said to me in class. You know, about if I thought of myself as American. And then when she was taking me to his office, about how all I know about is violence. Obviously he didn't do anything about it."

Nur giggled. "Kinzey. Maybe his parents are Russian or something. Maybe he's afraid of her."

"I can't believe she's married," Elham remarked.

"She is?" Nadia said incredulously.

"Yeah. Julie Falls is her daughter. That's a girl in our class."

"Anyway, now that my term paper is finished, I just have ten algebra problems to do, and then we can talk," Nur promised. She reached over for her algebra book.

"What am I going to do? I'm finished," Nadia complained.

"You can do my history." Elham started to hand her her book.

Nadia pushed it away. "No, thanks. I did enough world history last year. I'll just sit here quietly until you're done."

Twenty minutes later, Nur finished her algebra problems, and Elham's homework was completed soon after that.

"What time is it?" Nadia looked over at Nur's alarm clock. "Eight o'clock. So we have half an hour before we need to leave. What do you want to talk about?"

"I'm still so nervous about going back to school tomorrow," Elham confided. "In my mind, I already have a million excuses ready to tell my parents in the morning."

"What are you nervous about? I mean, what do you think is going to happen?" Nadia asked gently.

"I guess the same thing that happened last week except this time maybe worse," she admitted.

"Well," Nur sighed. "What can we do?"

"I know, but I don't want to get beat up."

"Well, I don't think that that would ever happen," Nadia consoled her. "I mean, they tease us and call us names and pull off our hijabs, but no one's ever done anything violent."

"I know, but I just keep thinking, what if?"

"When is your dad going over to talk to Mr. Kinzey?" Nur asked.

"Tomorrow after school," Elham answered. "And my mom and your mom and Mr. Rishovic are going to our old junior high school, Farid's school, on Thursday." Amir Rishovic was one of the members of the mosque.

"Maybe that'll help," Nadia suggested.

"I hope so. Sometimes I think that if everyone knew the real Islam—you know what I mean—then they wouldn't do stuff like this," Elham said. "But then I remember that in our high school kids are so immature. They probably don't even care."

"But education's important," Nadia agreed. "I mean, look at the Middle East right now. You have Sunni and Shia people killing each other every day over ignorance, that's all. And it's the same with Muslims and Christians."

"Anyway, I'm sure everything'll be okay tomorrow," Elham said, still not sounding very sure.

"It will be. We'll all stay together as much as possible this week and try not to be alone. And I'm sure everything will be fine," Nur agreed.

"Yeah, you're right," Elham said with a sigh. "Khalid and Hafsa were so nice to me today. I mean, Hafsa came to my locker at lunch so we could go to the cafeteria together. And then Khalid came to my locker right after school. Usually I go to my locker first and then we all meet at his. But today he was so nice."

"Yeah," Nur agreed. "I think Khalid's like Ibrahim. I mean, with Ibrahim, he teases me a lot and we fight a lot, but when I need something, he's always there for me."

"You know," Nadia said quietly. "I always wondered what it would be like to have an older brother. I mean, sometimes I wonder what it would be like if my brother Sergei was still alive."

"I'm sorry, Nadia," Elham said sympathetically.

"It's okay. I mean, I know it's sad, but I'm kind of glad I don't remember him. It makes it a little easier," Nadia admitted.

"I'm sure it's still hard, though," Nur said.

"Yeah, I hate war," she said tearfully.

Elham leaned over and gave her a hug. "Everybody does," she said.

"Anyway." Nadia pulled away and wiped the tears from her eyes. "Let's talk about something else."

"Like what?" Elham asked.

"I know," Nur answered promptly. "Saad."

Saad was walking past Nur's closed bedroom door when he heard his name mentioned. Curious as to what they were saying, he stopped outside the room to eavesdrop and see what was going on.

"You're still worried about him?" Elham asked.

"Yeah. I mean, I can't stop thinking about that phone number-- you know, the one I found written on his paper, the one to Saudi Arabia. I just know that OL has to be Osama bin Laden." Nur's voice was loud and clear.

Saad's eyes widened when he heard that.

"Why don't you try calling it and see?" Nadia suggested.

"Well, I thought about it, but what if it is him? What if the FBI traces the call and makes problems for my family?"

"It's not him, Nur, believe me," Nadia told her. "I mean, you think you can just pick up the phone and call Osama bin Laden, just like that? You think he gives out his phone number to just anybody? Of course not! If that was the case, they would have caught him a long time ago."

"Well, I don't think it's Osama bin Laden personally. Just maybe one of his contacts," Nur replied.

"I think you presented a pretty convincing case at lunch on Friday," Elham told her. "I mean, the beard thing and the speaking Arabic more. And his two friends from Saudi Arabia and the book on Arab nationalism. I don't know why your parents aren't more worried."

"I know!"

Saad couldn't believe what he was hearing.

"Well, what if you tell them about the phone number and the paper you found?" Elham asked.

"I can't, 'cause then they'll know that I went through his stuff."

"Oh, man!" Saad said to himself as Ibrahim started to walk down the hall. Saad signaled for him to be quiet and a second later, he joined him by the door.

"I have to agree with your parents," Nadia was saying. "I mean, with all of the stuff that you have, all of the so-called proof, there's a clear explanation for everything—one that clearly does not make Saad an extremist or a terrorist. And I like those explanations much better."

Ibrahim raised his eyebrows at his brother.

"Did you find anything else out over the weekend? Anything new?" Nadia continued.

"No," Nur admitted. "Saad worked all weekend. He wasn't really home much."

"Well, then I would just leave it," Nadia said. "Leave Saad alone. Now, let's talk about something else."

Saad and Ibrahim stopped listening and went next door into their bedroom. Ibrahim closed the door softly behind him.

"What was that all about?" he demanded.

"She is so going to pay for this," Saad declared.

"What? Pay for what?"

"You know, I can actually see in Nur's crazy, little mind how she would come up with the idea that I'm becoming an extremist," Saad continued ranting.

"She thinks you're an extremist?" Ibrahim asked incredulously.

"Yes! You heard her. Can you believe she went through my stuff?"

"Are you serious?"

"Yeah. She found the phone number I had written down of Adnan's brother in Saudi Arabia. And she thinks that OL—

Omar and Latifa—stands for Osama bin Laden."

Ibrahim couldn't help laughing. "Poor Nur!"

Saad laughed, too. "And not only that. She thinks 'cause I have a book on Arab nationalism, that makes me a terrorist. And she found some other paper somewhere. I don't know what it was. Probably just a grocery list with the word matches or something on it."

"Oh, man! She's the one who took our bag of Snickers," Ibrahim reasoned. "I knew it couldn't have been all finished. It was almost full."

"She is so going to pay for this," Saad repeated. "She thinks I'm a terrorist. Well, that's fine. I will be a terrorist."

Chapter 12

EARLY THURSDAY MORNING, MR. KARIM had left for work already. Mrs. Karim, Ibrahim, and Nur were seated at the kitchen counter eating breakfast. Mona was upstairs taking a shower.

"*Salaam-u-alaikum*," Saad said, joining them in the kitchen.

Nur's eyes widened when she saw him. He was wearing a dishdasha, the long white dress that Arab men wear in the Middle East, and he had on white pants underneath it. He was also wearing the cap for Muslim men and carrying prayer beads. With his new goatee, he looked like he had just stepped off a plane from Saudi Arabia.

"*Wa alaikum-a-salaam*," Mrs. Karim and Ibrahim replied together.

Saad sat down and poured himself a bowl of cereal and then added some milk.

"So anyway," Mrs. Karim was saying, "we're going over to the junior high school at 10:30 this morning to meet with Mrs. Ellis, the principal. I hope it goes better than the meeting with Mr. Kinzey did yesterday."

"Are you going to work like that?" Nur wanted to know, looking over at Saad.

"Like what?" he asked innocently.

"Like… that?"

"Actually I don't have work today. Just class."

They were silent for a minute before Saad spoke up. "Mom, I'd like some juice," he said.

"Sure." She went over to the refrigerator and poured him a glass of orange juice. "Anyone else want any?"

Ibrahim and Nur shook their heads, and Mrs. Karim put the juice away. She brought Saad his glass, and he immediately took a drink without saying another word.

"Can you at least say thank you?" Nur demanded.

"Why should I say thank you?" Saad replied. "It's her job."

"It's her job?" Nur repeated incredulously. "It is not her job! You have two legs!"

"But I don't do things like that." He calmly continued to eat his cereal. "I'm a man, she's a woman."

Mrs. Karim could not believe her ears. This was Saad? He had to be just joking. She looked closely at him. No, he was completely serious.

"Another thing, Nur," Saad added. "I would appreciate it if you start wearing your hijab around me, out of respect." Again, he sounded completely serious.

"But you're my brother," she protested. "I don't have to wear it around you."

"Of course, you don't have to. But it's more respectful since I am your older brother. And it's more religious," he told her.

Nur, seemingly in shock and at a loss for words, simply took her empty bowl and glass over to the sink. She rinsed them out and put them in the dishwasher and then silently left the room. She knew that if she stayed, she would probably explode and say some things she would later regret. Where in the world did he come up with this garbage? Who was he hanging out with that was teaching him this stuff? Were there really people like that in Ames, Iowa?

"Saad, are you okay? Mrs. Karim asked, sounding concerned. "Is there anything you want to talk about?"

"No," he said simply, continuing to eat.

"Okay, well, I'm going to go check on Mona." She stood up and left the kitchen.

Saad and Ibrahim could hardly contain themselves.

"Did you see the look on her face?" Saad demanded quietly.

"Priceless!" his brother agreed.

"This is nothing," Saad added. "Just wait until the phone call this afternoon."

⌒

After school that day, Nur and Ibrahim sat in the family room talking to their mother about her meeting at the junior high school that morning.

"Mrs. Ellis was really nice," Mrs. Karim told them. "You know, with all of the years you kids spent at that school, I can't believe I never met her before."

"What did she say?" Ibrahim asked.

"She said she always felt so bad about the way kids treated you when you played basketball," she told Nur.

"Yeah, she was really nice. She used to come over to me in the hall and tell me congratulations and stuff like that when I played good," Nur recalled. "And I remember during one game, when I missed a free throw and someone from our side shouted something like 'stupid Arab,' she called security to take them out of the gym. It was so nice of her."

"Huh. Anyway, then she said that unfortunately she didn't think anything would make a difference because of the way junior high students are. She said it wasn't just Muslims who are targeted but anyone seen as different or vulnerable. But she *was* interested in having one of the imams talk to the teachers. And when I told her what Mr. Kinzey said about favoring Islam over other religions, she said she didn't think that was a problem and that if anyone complained, she would try to accommodate them. She said she wasn't concerned that students or parents of other religions would complain, but more that the Christian parents would. She was really nice," Mrs. Karim repeated.

The day before Mr. AlAmery and two other mosque members had met with Mr. Kinzey at the high school. He was reluctant to allow the Islamic center to organize a talk for the teachers about Islam. He had accepted their points, but had stated that he was concerned that parents would complain that they were favoring one religion over another, and then they would have to organize talks to the teachers about all the different religions represented at the high school.

"Wow, that's good," Ibrahim said.

"Yeah," their mother agreed. "And the group that went to West Des Moines High School said the principal was really nice and interested. So we're making some headway."

Just then they heard the front door open, and a minute later Saad joined them in the family room. He was still wearing the dishdasha and cap and carrying the prayer beads.

"*Salaam-u-alaikum*," he greeted them, sitting down on the floor. He set his bag of books down next to him.

"*Wa alaikum-a-salaam*," Ibrahim and Mrs. Karim replied.

"How were your classes today?" Mrs. Karim added.

"Okay," he answered.

"Do you have to work tonight?" she asked.

"No, I have the day off. Actually, I'm off until the weekend." He paused. "That's good because I've been thinking about quitting and finding a different job."

"Why? You've worked there almost three years now."

"Yeah, but the bookstore is so westernized. It's so corrupt. I mean, they play rock music a lot, and there's always teenagers hanging out there, girls wearing skimpy clothes and holding hands with different boys every week. And I'm just tired of it," he explained, trying to sound disgusted.

"Yes, but every place is like that," Mrs. Karim pointed out.

"Well, and the other thing is, they sell a lot of indecent books—about sex and stuff. And indecent movies and music. And they have a lot of anti-Islam books—Salman Rushdie and stuff like that. How can I work there, knowing that my paycheck comes from this garbage?"

"So where do you think you can find a job that would be better?"

Saad shrugged his shoulders. "I don't know. Maybe in an office or delivering pizza." The last choice had just come to him.

"But pizza places don't use halal meat, and they use pork. And some of them serve alcohol," Mrs. Karim pointed out.

"Well, I don't know." Saad turned to his sister to try to change the subject. He hadn't expected his mother to go on and on about the job like that. "Thank you for listening to what I said this morning and wearing your hijab around me. You look really nice."

"Actually I just got home. I just didn't take it off yet," Nur informed him. She reached up to remove it.

"No, leave it please," he requested.

"Well, if I have to always leave it on around you, then I'm just going to stay in my room." She sounded like she was ready to cry. "Because I want to be comfortable in my own house."

Saad shrugged his shoulders. He didn't know what to say, but he hoped he wasn't going overboard. Then he remembered what he had heard the other night, how she had gone through his things, and he knew his younger sister needed to be taught a lesson.

"Oh, shoot, I almost forgot," Ibrahim said suddenly, standing up. "I have this book I need to give back to Khalid, and I told him I would drop it off today."

"I think Elham said Khalid's working today," Nur informed him.

He looked over at the clock. "Yeah, that's why I need to drop it off now." He disappeared down the hall and returned a minute later carrying a book. "I'll be back in a few minutes."

After Ibrahim left, Nur turned back to her mother. "So someone's going to talk to the junior high teachers, you said?" She didn't want to listen to Saad anymore.

"Yeah," Mrs. Karim replied. "I gave her a business card from the mosque, and she said she was going to call one of the imams."

"Can I use your phone?" Saad interrupted, turning to his mother. "I need to make an overseas phone call. I'll pay for it."

"Sure. Where are you calling?" his mother asked.

"Saudi Arabia," Saad said with a completely straight face. "I need to talk to Adnan's brother about a possible business deal. And he said midnight there is a good time to call, which is now." He stood up.

"What kind of business deal?"

"He designs computer websites for Islamic centers and organizations in the Gulf countries. And he wants to break into the market here in North America."

"So how would you be helping him? Why not Adnan?"

"Well, because I know more about designing websites, and I was going to talk to our Islamic center to start with to see if they'd be interested in using his company." He felt so guilty lying to his mother. "And then maybe he might let me work for him here."

"Okay." Mrs. Karim shrugged her shoulders. "Just be careful."

Nur stood up, too. "Yeah, I think I need to start my homework." She followed her brother down the hallway.

Saad took the cordless telephone from his parents' bedroom into his. He closed the door partway.

Meanwhile, Nur wandered into her bedroom and sat down at the desk to start her homework. "How can I concentrate at a time like this?" she asked herself.

A minute later she heard Saad's voice as he spoke loudly on the telephone. "*Allo, salaam-u-alaikum!*" He was practically shouting. "*Ayman akhi! Kaif halkum? Hatha Saad, Saad min America! Saad ibn Ahmed, min America!*"

"Why is Saad shouting?" Mona demanded. She was sitting on the bed reading. "And who's Ayman?"

"I don't know," Nur answered brusquely.

Saad continued to speak loudly in Arabic. "What's going on? Oh, good, good, good. How is he? His kidneys are doing better? Good, good, good. What's the new plan? *Yaani*, the mosque here is just small, just a small city…"

Ibrahim and Khalid were on the other end. They could hardly contain their laughter.

Nur, too, could only sit and listen in shock. Ayman? How is he? What's the new plan? It was almost too obvious… I mean, you would think there would be code names and… unless it was too obvious.

"That rat," Nur said softly to herself. "He must have heard us talking about him and now this is all an act." Of course, it all made sense. The number that just happened to belong to someone in Saudi Arabia with the initials OL, that just happened to be written on a paper right on top of his desk. The dishdasha and the sobha, the phone call to someone in Saudi Arabia.

"Well, two can play this game," Nur swore to herself. "Boy, is he going to pay."

⌒

Half an hour later, Nur was sitting on her parents' bed, talking on the phone to Elham.

"So you think—" Elham cut off for a second. "Sorry, Farid was just in here. Anyway, so you think he heard us talking?" she asked softly.

"He must have," Nur replied. "I mean, he's got to be acting. Don't you think it's too obvious? I mean, Ayman?"

"Well, Ayman's just a name. It doesn't have to mean Ayman, Osama's friend. I have an uncle named Ayman."

"Well, you have a million uncles, Elham. You probably have one named Osama, too."

"No. But anyway, you're probably right. I mean, the kidney thing does sound a little obvious. Plus, all of a sudden he just happens to start wearing a dishdasha and making you wear hijab around him, talking about how corrupt the bookstore is. I'm sure you're right. I'm sure he's just acting," Elham agreed. "Oh, man, I can see why you're so annoyed."

"So... I have a plan. Do you want to work with me on it?" Nur said mischievously.

"Well, tell me the plan first, and I'll see."

"Okay, one day after school we'll just try to make him believe we're going to call the FBI and report him," Nur told her.

"Hmmm, it sounds interesting. Tell me more."

"Okay. We'll plan the day, and then we'll sit next to their wall in my room, and I'll be like, what do I do? What do I do? And you'll be like, you have to call the FBI, you have to. He's a terrorist. You have to report him. And we'll just go on like that until he breaks."

"What if he doesn't?"

"He will. I'm sure he will."

Chapter 13

For the rest of that week, Ibrahim continued to see Christy briefly after school at their lockers. They didn't go out again, just hung out around the school building together for a few minutes. They didn't make arrangements for another date until Friday.

That day after school, as if on cue, Christy appeared at his locker. She had another girl with her this time.

"Hey, boyfriend," she said flirtatiously.

"Hi, Christy," Ibrahim replied.

"What do you want to do today? It's Friday!"

"I don't care. What do you want to do?"

"Well, my parents are gone until tonight, and Greg has basketball practice. So what if we go over to my house?" she suggested.

"Okay," he agreed. "But I have to be home by 5:30 PM."

"That's fine. This is my friend Melissa. She can drive us."

The three of them headed out to the parking lot to Melissa's SUV and climbed inside.

"So, are you a cheerleader, too?" Ibrahim asked from the backseat.

"Yeah," Melissa answered.

"When do you guys have practice?"

"Usually after school," Christy told him. "This is our last week off before we have to start practicing for basketball season. So we're not going to be able to see each other that much after this weekend."

"Are you coming to the party tonight?" Melissa asked.

"What party?" Ibrahim replied.

"Katie, one of the other cheerleaders, is having a party at her place. Her parents are gone for the weekend," Christy explained. "Can you come?"

"Probably not. I think I need to help my dad with some stuff," Ibrahim lied.

"On a Friday night?"

"Yeah," he replied. "Sorry."

A few minutes later, Melissa drove into a neighborhood of large, new houses. After a couple of turns, they pulled up in front of a huge, two-story brick house with an attached three-car garage.

"This is it," Christy announced.

"Will your brother be home by 5:00 PM?" Ibrahim asked, trying not to appear too awed. He had never been to such a large house.

"Probably not," she admitted, turning to her friend. "Mel lives right down the street. Can you drive Ibrahim home?"

Melissa nodded. "Sure. Should I just be back at 5:00 PM?"

"That'd be great," he agreed.

"Okay, see you then. Have fun." She smiled knowingly at Christy.

Christy led Ibrahim to the front door, and they entered into a large foyer with a crystal chandelier. From the doorway, you could see through the glass patio doors in the family room that led to the back, complete with a large porch and an in-ground swimming pool.

"Wow, nice house," he commented.

She shrugged. "It's okay. We'll go up to my room in a minute. I just want to check the phone messages, see if my parents called."

She walked over to the telephone, and a minute later Ibrahim heard a woman's voice.

"Hi, kids. It's about 2:30 PM. We're going to stay for the dinner here at 6:00 PM and then we'll leave after that, so we won't be home until late, probably around 11:00 PM. Leave a note if you go out tonight, and just have a good time. Bye."

"They're at a dental conference in Kansas City," Christy explained to Ibrahim. "Anyway, let's go up to my room." She reached for his hand.

"I don't think that's a good idea, Christy," Ibrahim replied.

"What do you mean?"

"Well, we can just hang out here, maybe watch a movie or something," he suggested.

"Watch a movie now?" She sounded surprised.

"Well, watch a little television. Why not?" He sat down on the couch.

Christy shrugged her shoulders. "Whatever. Do you want something to drink? My dad has some beer in the refrigerator," she said mischievously.

"I don't drink," Ibrahim replied.

"Really? Never?"

"No."

"Well, do you want a Pepsi or something?" she offered.

"Sure, thanks."

Christy disappeared into the kitchen and returned a minute later with two cans of Sprite. "It's all I could find," she explained, joining him on the couch.

"That's okay. So…"

"So… don't you want to kiss me?"

"No, that's okay. We can just hang out and talk," Ibrahim answered.

"All we do is talk," Christy complained. "Let's do something fun." She moved a little closer to him, so their legs were touching, and then put her hand on his arm.

"Talking and getting to know each other is fun."

"Kissing is fun, too."

"I don't want to kiss," he told her.

"But we like each other. That's what couples do." By this time, she was practically on top of him. She started to put her hand under his t-shirt and kiss his neck.

Ibrahim immediately pulled away. "Christy!"

"What? Don't be such a prude. Live a little. If you're not comfortable here, we can go up to my room." She looked at him with her big blue eyes.

"I'm not a prude. I just think it's too soon."

"Well, not really. With my last boyfriend, he started kissing me right away." Christy leaned back on the couch and shrugged her shoulders.

"Well, I'm not your last boyfriend," Ibrahim said defensively.

"So you don't like me?"

"No, I do like you, Christy. But not that much." He stood up.

"Ibrahim, don't be mad," she pleaded. "I really like you."

"Me, too," he said.

"Okay," she agreed. "We can wait. I don't care about that stuff. I just thought you would want to."

"Anyway, I think I should go," Ibrahim said.

Christy took his hand and pulled it so he ended up sitting back next to her on the couch, practically on her lap. "Ibrahim, just wait," she said, putting her hand on his leg.

He stood back up. "No, I'm going to go."

"I don't know why you're getting so mad." She pouted.

"I'm not mad. I'll call you, okay?"

"Whatever." Christy rolled her eyes.

Ibrahim sighed. "Well, I'm sorry you don't understand. I will call you… if you want me to."

"Of course, I want you to. I want to be your girlfriend. But I also want to have fun. So don't be mad at me if I go to this party tonight," she told him honestly.

Ibrahim couldn't believe his ears. "Whatever. See you later." He began walking toward the front door.

"Do you want me to call Melissa?" she called after him.

"No, that's okay."

"So how will you get home?"

"I'll walk or take the bus," he replied.

"Are you mad?" she asked. "Are we breaking up?"

Ibrahim sighed and turned back around. "No, we're not breaking up. I'll call you, okay?" He picked up his backpack.

"Will you be mad at me if I hook up with someone at the party tonight? Because we're not really boyfriend and girlfriend right now."

"Whatever."

Ibrahim walked out the front door. He headed out of the wealthy neighborhood to one of the main streets where he found a bus stop. When the city bus pulled up, he climbed inside and found a seat.

He couldn't believe how stupid he felt. Everyone was right, she had just used him. He had thought it would be so cool to have a girlfriend. He couldn't believe the stuff he had done that week—going out with a girl, touching and kissing her, and missing a lot of prayers. But it had felt really good. Just looking back to the last few days, he thought how nice it was to walk with her, the smell of her hair, the warmth of her hand. Why was all of this wrong? It didn't seem possible. Okay, missing the prayers, yes, that was wrong. But everything else?

The bus pulled up to a stop near the Karims' house, and Ibrahim got off and walked the rest of the way. When he arrived home, he found Nur and Mona in the family room reading.

"Where is everyone?" Ibrahim asked.

"Mom just got home. She's taking a shower. Daddy's not home yet, and Saad's at work," Nur reported. "Khalid called twice for you. I thought you weren't going to be back until later, so I told him to call back tonight."

"Okay. Well, maybe I'll call him now." Ibrahim put down his backpack. He felt like talking to someone. "Hey, do you guys mind if I have a little privacy?"

"Wow, you never ask so nicely," Nur said in surprise. She gathered up her books. "Come on, Mona. Let's go to the bedroom."

Mona stood up obediently, still reading, and followed her sister down the hallway without closing her book for a second.

Ibrahim picked up the telephone and quickly dialed the AlAmery's number. Luckily, Khalid himself answered.

"Hello?" he said.

"Hi, Khalid, it's me."

"Hey, Ibrahim. Where were you?"

"Just out for a little while," Ibrahim hedged. "What are you doing? Can I come over for a few minutes?"

"Yeah, but I'm going to the mosque with my dad at 5:00 PM," Khalid replied.

Ibrahim looked at the clock. It was 4:15 PM. "Yeah, that's fine," he agreed. "I'll be there in a minute."

"Okay. Bye."

Ibrahim hung up the phone as his mother entered the room.

"Hi, Ibrahim. How was school?" she greeted him.

"It was okay. It was good. How was work?" he replied.

"Busy." She sat down in the recliner and leaned back. Mrs. Karim was a nurse at one of the local hospitals. She worked in the obstetrics department, where she had worked for the last ten years. She had come to the United States with her family when she was seventeen years old, to escape the Palestinian territories. She had been unable to finish high school because, as the oldest child, she needed to work and help support her family after their arrival in the US. Later, she had studied English, received her GED, and attended nursing school. She met her husband through mutual friends and family when she was in her last year of school. They had married and settled down in Ames, then Des Moines. Her parents and brothers now lived outside Chicago.

"Busy, huh? Lots of babies?" Ibrahim asked.

She smiled. "Lots of people in labor. Only one baby so far, although I think another one came right after I left."

"Say, Mom, I'm going to run over to Khalid's for a little while," Ibrahim said. "I'll be home by 5:00 PM, and then Nur and I can make dinner."

"Well, thank you, azizi. Go ahead, but that's okay. I just need to rest a little and then I'll get started."

"Mother," he insisted. "I'll be back by 5:00 PM, and we'll do it. Don't go in the kitchen," he said threateningly. He went over and kissed his mother on the cheek. "See you in a little while."

Ibrahim hurriedly slipped on some sandals and went out the front door and across the street where Khalid was waiting for him on their front steps.

"Hey," Khalid said, standing up.

"Hey," Ibrahim replied. "You want to just sit out here?"

"Sure. So..." Khalid began as they sat down on the steps. "I saw you leaving school today with that cheerleader and her friend."

"Oh." Ibrahim seemed embarrassed.

Khalid was silent for a minute. "So what's going on?" he asked finally. "I mean, I thought we had talked about that."

"I messed up," Ibrahim admitted. "Big time. I mean, I guess I thought everything would be okay, you know, that nothing would happen. It would just be like I had a girlfriend and maybe I'd be able to hang out with all of the cool guys. But," he sighed, "of course, that's not what she wanted. I feel really stupid."

"Did you do anything?"

"No," he assured his friend. "Almost. But, no. And I guess I should have expected that. I mean, the first time we went out together, I don't know, almost right away she tried to kiss me."

"Huh."

"I mean, I didn't expect it like that. I thought we would hold hands and go places together, and she would be, like, my girl-friend, you know. But it wasn't like that. I feel really stupid," Ibrahim said again.

Khalid shrugged his shoulders. "It's okay," he said. "People make mistakes."

Ibrahim sighed again. "I guess." He didn't say anything for a minute and then added, "But, Khalid, before today… I mean, before she tried to, you know… it was kind of nice. I mean, it kind of felt good to be with a girl, you know, walking and talking and stuff."

"Well, Ibrahim, I think you need to decide what you want. I mean, don't you see now why having a girlfriend is haram?"

"I guess."

"Well, this is why. You were with a girl for a week and you held hands and kissed. And you liked it. That's why it's haram. Of course, Allah knows it's nice and it makes you want more. That's why you shouldn't be alone with a girl to begin with," Khalid lectured.

"I know."

"Well, if you know, then you need to stop it."

"I know, Khalid, I know!" Ibrahim said angrily. "Stop saying I told you so."

"I'm not saying I told you so. I'm saying, decide what you want. Because the way I see right now, you're doing just like what you said the other day about Christians who drink and stuff and then go to church the next day."

"I'm not drinking," he said defensively.

"It's the same thing, Ibrahim," Khalid told him.

"Well, anyway, I'm not going to call her," Ibrahim said. "It's finished."

"Good. I hope so." He paused. "You know, Ibrahim, I don't mean to lecture. I mean, I told you the other day, sometimes I feel the same way, like, how nice it would be to have a girlfriend and be so cool."

"So what stops you? I mean, I know it's wrong, but…"

"Well, I wonder how I would feel if it was Elham. Or I wonder how I would feel in ten years when I get married if I knew that my wife had gone out with other boys," Khalid said. "Because all of this stuff is wrong for both men and women. I mean, I know a lot of Muslim men who do this stuff but expect women not to. But that's wrong. We're all equal and that's it."

"Yeah, but what difference does it make now? I'm not going to get married for a long time."

"But it doesn't matter if you go out with, or kiss, or do other stuff with a girl once or fifty times, ten years before you get married or the day before. You know it's wrong, you know it's haram."

"I know. And I'm never going to do anything like that again. Even though I thought it was nice, I know it's wrong. I just need more self control." Ibrahim paused. "Anyway, I should go home.

My mom had a busy day at work, and I told her that Nur and I would make dinner."

"Wow, that's nice of you," Khalid replied.

"Yeah we do it sometimes." Ibrahim shrugged. "It's no big deal. Usually we just have pizza or something." He grinned. "I left it up to Nur one day, and we ended up with boiled eggs. Boy, did she get a lecture that night! My dad made her spend that weekend in the kitchen with my mom, learning how to cook."

Khalid laughed. "Does she cook now?"

"Kind of. She makes good falafel. And her kabob's okay. It's better than mine," he admitted. "About all I make is pizza."

"Pizza's okay."

"Yeah, it's easy." Ibrahim stood up. "Anyway, thanks for everything, Khalid."

"You're welcome." Khalid stood up, too. "Call me tomorrow. Or even tonight. I'll be home by 7:00 PM."

"Sure."

Khalid watched his friend walk back across the street and disappear inside his house. He noticed their older neighbors sitting on their front porch, enjoying the nice fall day.

"Hi, Mr. and Mrs. Kelly!" he called over to them, waving.

"Hi, Khalid!" Mr. Kelly replied as his wife smiled. "Enjoying the nice weather?"

"Yeah, it's really nice today," Khalid agreed before heading back inside his house. He found Farid in the family room using the computer. Elham was in her bedroom. Before he could say anything, the telephone rang.

"I'll get it!" Farid said, picking up the receiver next to the computer. "Hello?" he said.

"Hello, is Hassan AlAmery in please?" the man on the other end asked politely.

"Actually, no. He's at work. May I take a message?" Farid, assuming it was a telemarketer, didn't even bother to grab a pen.

"Is this a family member?" the man asked as Khalid entered the family room.

"Yeah, this is his son," Farid replied.

"Well, my name is Greg Wilson. I'm calling from the FBI."

"Um, just a minute," Farid interrupted as soon as he heard that. "I'll let you talk to my older brother." He handed the phone to Khalid and mouthed, "The FBI. Asking for Dad."

Khalid raised his eyebrows in surprise. "Hello?" he said.

"Hi, this is Greg Wilson. I'm calling from the FBI," he repeated. "I just have some questions for your father, who, I understand, is Hassan AlAmery."

"Yes, but he's at work right now. Do you want to leave a message?" Khalid asked, reaching for the pen and pad of paper they kept by the telephone.

"Yes, I'll give you my phone number. Have him call me at his earliest convenience," Mr. Wilson requested. "I just have a few questions for him."

"A few questions about what?"

"I'll talk to him when he calls." He proceeded to give Khalid the phone number and then added, "I'll be here until 6:00 PM today. And then tomorrow from 9:00 AM to 6:00 PM again."

"Okay. Probably he can call you today." Khalid looked up at the wall clock. It was 4:40 PM. "He should be home in a few minutes."

"Great. Thank you very much."

Khalid hung up the phone and turned to his younger brother. "That was the FBI," he told him.

"I know. What'd they want with Dad?" Farid demanded.

"I don't know. He wouldn't tell me. He just gave me his phone number and said to have Dad call him."

"I wonder why. I mean, I hope everything's okay."

"Yeah, I'm sure it's nothing." Khalid tried to sound reassuring.

"Where's Mom?" Farid asked.

"She left a note. She had to interpret for a doctor's appointment at 3:30 PM, and she said she'd be home around 5:00 PM," Khalid replied.

Five minutes later, the door from the garage opened, and Mr. AlAmery entered. He took off his shoes and joined his sons who were anxiously waiting for him in the family room.

"*Salaam*," he greeted them.

"*Salaam*," they replied together.

"Mom had an appointment at 3:30 PM," Khalid told him. "And Elham's in her room."

"Great. That's fine."

"And I think Mom already made dinner," Farid added.

"Okay. I'm going to go take a shower, and then we'll go to the mosque," Mr. AlAmery said.

"Uh, Dad, before you go," Khalid spoke up. "Right before you got home, the phone rang, and it was the FBI. They wanted to talk to you. I have the phone number here."

"The FBI? They wanted to talk to me?" He sat down in a chair.

"Yeah. I answered the phone, and it was this man, and when he said he was from the FBI, I gave the phone to Khalid," Farid said.

"And I have his name and phone number here. He said he'd be there until 6:00 PM, so you still have time." Khalid handed his father the paper with the name and telephone number on it. "And he seemed nice."

Mr. AlAmery looked up at the clock. It was 4:25 PM now. "All right. Well, I'll call him now," he said, reaching for the piece of paper. He dialed the phone number that Khalid had written down. Two rings later, a man's voice picked up.

"This is Greg," he said.

"Hello, is this Greg Wilson?" Mr. AlAmery asked.

"Yes, it is."

"This is Hassan AlAmery. My son said you called and needed to talk to me?"

"Yes, thank you for calling me back," Mr. Wilson replied politely. "First of all, you speak Arabic, correct?"

"Yes."

"Are you comfortable with English or would you like an interpreter?"

Mr. AlAmery shrugged. "No, I think English is okay. Did you have some questions?"

"Actually, I do. But we need to set up a time when we can meet. How's Monday afternoon, like around this time?" the FBI agent suggested.

"I guess."

"You don't have to. It's completely voluntary."

"No, it's okay."

"Okay, then. Do you know where our office in Des Moines is?" He proceeded to give him the address and telephone number and then added, "So I'll see you here on Monday around 4:30 PM."

"Okay." Mr. AlAmery hung up the phone.

"What did he want, Dad?" Khalid asked.

"I'm not sure," Mr. AlAmery answered, trying to hide his concern. "I guess we'll find out on Monday."

Chapter 14

LATER THAT EVENING, ELHAM was sitting in her room reading through the final draft of her term paper. Although Nur had turned hers in early, this time it was Elham who had procrastinated until the end. She had just printed it off the computer a few minutes ago, but she was having a difficult time concentrating on the paper. She looked at the clock again. It was only 7:50.

One of the girls who had taunted her last week was in her English class. Her name was Beth Ferris. She was also one of the girls who had bothered Khalid at Super Foods. She had been absent from class the entire week, and that day Elham had heard a couple of girls saying some really mean things about her. Despite the way she had treated her, Elham could not help feeling sorry for her. Apparently she should be a sophomore, but she had missed so many classes last year that she was kept back.

On a whim, Elham had thought about trying to call her. She had even asked one of her classmates for her phone number. Was she crazy to do something like that after everything that had happened? She wondered. She decided to talk it over with Nadia. Of all her friends, Nadia was the best person to give advice.

Elham went out to the family room to get the telephone. Her parents were still at the mosque. She took the telephone receiver into her room and dialed Nadia's number. Luckily, Nadia herself answered.

"Hello?" she said.

"Hi, Nadia. It's me, Elham."

"Hey! What's up?"

"I have a question. Actually I just need some advice."

"Okay. Go ahead."

"Well, one of the girls who bothered me last week, she's in my English class. And she hasn't been here all week. And anyway, today I heard these girls in class talking about her. Supposedly they're her friends, but they were saying really mean things about her. Like, she's stupid because she failed ninth grade. They were calling her mother names, and saying she did drugs and stuff like that."

"Huh. Well, you're right. That's not very nice."

"Yeah, I know. So, I mean, maybe she just doesn't like school. She has a job. I heard her talking about it one day," Elham told her.

"Hmmm. Well, what's your point, though? I mean…" Nadia's voice drifted off.

"Well, I was thinking about calling her."

"Why?"

"I don't know. To apologize maybe," Elham said, sounding uncertain.

"Why do you need to apologize?" Nadia demanded.

"I don't know. I just feel bad for her. I just want to let her know that I'm not mad about what happened."

Nadia's voice filled with doubt. "I don't know, Elham. I don't know if that's such a good idea. Besides, how do you know her phone number?"

"I asked one of the girls in my class for it," Elham answered. "I guess, I'm just worried that maybe if I call her she'll get mad or upset."

"Well, I don't think she will. I mean, it's a really nice thing for you to do."

"Thanks. I just think that maybe she's embarrassed to go back to school after what happened. Plus, I think she was in detention until Monday. I don't know after that."

"Maybe you're right. Maybe if you do call her and just talk to her, maybe it'll make her feel better. At least, it's not going to hurt anything. The worst thing that can happen is that she can hang up on you or get mad," Nadia advised.

"Yeah, that's true. You're right. Okay, maybe I will." Elham sounded more confident.

"That's such a nice thing to do, Elham. You're so amazing."

"Thanks."

"And if you do call her," Nadia added, "let me know how things go."

"I will. And thanks for the advice. I knew you were the right person to call."

"No problem."

"I'll talk to you later." Elham hung up the phone. She sat on her bed for a minute, thinking, before reaching for her geometry notebook to look up the phone number she had written down inside. Before she could change her mind, she quickly dialed the number. An older woman answered the telephone. "Hello?" she said.

"Hello, is Beth there?" Elham asked.

"Yes, just a minute." There was a loud thunk as she put the phone down and called out, "Beth, phone for you! And don't forget to stay in here."

"Hello?" the teenaged girl said a minute later.

"Hi, Beth. It's Elham—Elham AlAmery from your English class."

"What do you want? And how'd you get my phone number?"

"I got it from Rachel, in our English class. And I just wanted to call because you haven't been in class for a while. I mean, since Thanksgiving," Elham told her.

"Yeah, well, I've missed class lots of times, and you never called before," Beth said bitterly.

"I know. I guess I felt really bad after everything that happened last week."

"Well, you should. I spent five days in juvenile detention, thanks to you."

"It wasn't because of me. Everything you did, it was your decision to do. I mean, you had a choice."

"Whatever. Anyway, what do you want?" Beth repeated.

"Well, I just wanted to make sure everything's okay and see if you want any English assignments or anything. Actually we didn't really have any this week, just the term paper that's due on Monday," Elham informed her.

"So what?"

"Well, if you want to meet somewhere this weekend, we can go over it," Elham said. "There's this really nice coffee shop called Sabrina's that's close to the mo—close to where I live. I like to go there sometimes in the afternoon and read 'cause it's so quiet. And then I can just walk home. Do you want to meet me there tomorrow morning, maybe around 10:00?"

"No."

"Why not?"

"Because. I don't want to. And besides, I'm not going to school anymore," Beth informed her.

"Come anyway," Elham persisted. "It's a really nice coffee shop. I'm sure you'll like it."

"No."

"Okay, well, if you want I can help you with your term paper. I bet if you ask Mr. Collins, he'll give you an extension," Elham suggested.

"You think everything is so easy, don't you? Just ask the teacher, and they'll do whatever you want. Well, it's not that easy. Listen, I've got to go. Bye." Beth hung up the phone.

Elham hung up, too, and just sat in silence for a minute.

⌒

The next morning, Elham walked down to Sabrina's Coffee Shop for a little while. She wanted to go there anyway, and she still hoped that Beth would come. She couldn't explain why, but she really wanted to talk to her, to see why she had done what she did the week before.

Elham knew the girls who worked there because she, Nur, and Nadia were all frequent customers. She ordered a hot chocolate and then sat down at one of the tables to read. She was reading the book *The Alchemist*. A few minutes later, just as she had hoped, Beth came in and sat down in the chair across from her.

"So why did you really call me last night?" Beth demanded without even saying hello.

Elham put down her book. "Really? Because I just wanted to know why you did all of the stuff that you did. Why you hate Muslims so much. But last night I was afraid to ask."

"Because you're all terrorists."

"Don't be crazy. Do I look like a terrorist?"

"Well, you all love Osama bin Laden. You hate America," Beth accused.

"My family and I love America. It was the American soldiers that saved my parents from being killed by Saddam Hussein. And who took them across the border where they were safe. And it was the American government that brought us all here," Elham told her. "We don't hate America. Actually, Osama bin Laden and his stupid Al Qaeda friends are killing all of my people right now in Iraq. I hate him."

"Whatever." Beth rolled her eyes.

Elham sighed. "Anyway, open your mind a little. You have to have a reason. You can't just make a generalized broad accusation like that, that all Muslims are terrorists and hate America. Do you know bad Muslims? I mean, did somebody here do something to you?"

"No. It's just…I hate my life. And I always see you guys hanging out together, exclusively, like the popular crowd except you're Muslims only. And you're dressed different and always laughing and stuff."

"We don't dress different. Other then the scarves, we dress just like everyone else. And not all of us even wear scarves," Elham replied. "And I guess I never really thought about it, but I guess we do really just hang out together."

"Yeah, you do."

"Huh. I never really paid attention."

"Anyway, Mike, one of the guys that was with me with you, and then at the store with your brother, he just likes to make trouble. And the rest of us, we just wanted to teach you guys a lesson," Beth told her honestly.

"Believe me, we don't mean to be exclusive. It's just that a lot of people make fun of us and stuff, so we usually just stick together," Elham tried to explain.

"Maybe they wouldn't make fun of you if you tried to have different friends."

"I guess I never really thought about it," Elham repeated. "But you're right." She paused. "You know, you're really smart. I mean, you pick up on things really easy. How come you don't try do better in school?"

"I hate school. I hate studying. I hate the teachers. I hate everything about it."

"Well, I can help you with it," Elham offered. "I help my friend Nur. She doesn't like school either."

"Why would you want to help me?"

"Because… you're nice. And besides, you helped me a lot today. You helped me realize why maybe some people bother us and now that I know that, I can do something about it. Because really last week, I just wanted to quit school and move. I was crying every day about it."

"I'm sorry." Beth actually sounded sympathetic.

"Anyway, promise me that you'll come to school on Monday. And I promise that I'll help you with the paper," Elham told her.

"We'll see."

"Okay. We'll see is better than no."

Beth smiled for the first time.

"How come you said you hate your life? A little while ago you said you hate your life," Elham reminded her."

"Oh, never mind. Anyway—" She pushed back her chair. "I need to go.'"

"Why? I'm having a good time with you."

"I have to work tonight."

"Okay. Look, I'm sorry you spent five days in juvenile detention, but you really should have told one of us about the friends thing instead of doing all the stuff you did."

"Anyway, I need to go." Beth stood up and left the coffee shop.

After she left, Elham sat at her table for a few minutes just to think. She had never really paid attention to the fact that all of her close friends were Muslim. Of course, she had a few friends who were non-Muslims, but they weren't really close. As she sipped her hot chocolate, she vowed to do better, to reach out more to non-Muslim students, people like Beth.

"Maybe it won't change anything," she said to herself. "But maybe it will."

Chapter 15

MONDAY WAS THE BIG DAY FOR NUR. She would be putting all of her acting skills to the test, hopefully to give Saad a taste of his own medicine. She and Elham had rehearsed the whole scene in their minds and over the phone again and again, and they thought they were finally ready.

After school, Mona had gone over to visit Nadia's sister Lena for a while, and Elham was hanging out with Nur in her bedroom. They sat on Nur's bed, leaning against the wall that separated their bedroom from that of Saad and Ibrahim's. Nur knew that Saad was in his room doing homework, but she wasn't sure about Ibrahim.

"Ready?" Nur asked quietly.

Elham smiled nervously. "I think so."

Nur took a deep breath. "I don't know what to do, Elham," she said loudly, trying to sound tearful. "I mean, I don't know what's going on with my brother. I just don't know what to do anymore."

Ibrahim was sitting on his bed by the wall, starting his homework. "Saad," he said softly. "Come here." He signaled for his brother to join him.

"I know, Nur. I don't know what to tell you," Elham said. "But what you heard last week… I mean, the phone call… I mean, there's no other explanation for it."

"I know. So what do I do?" Nur moaned.

"Well, Nur, I know he's your brother, but maybe he's working with Al Qaeda. I mean, obviously he is. And maybe they're planning another attack here in America. Maybe he's helping them plan an attack right here in Des Moines. Who knows? We have tall buildings. You have to report your concerns. You *have* to. It's your duty as an American," Elham insisted.

"Elham's imagination is just as bad as Nur's," Saad thought. "They've been hanging around each other way too much."

"I can't, Elham, I can't. I can't report my own brother," Nur said. "What if they arrest him? What if they send him to Guantanomo or Afghanistan or one of those other torture camps? I could never live with myself."

"I'm sure they're not going to arrest him. They'll just talk to him, question him. If he knows something, he'll tell them, and they'll be happy. If he doesn't, then that's great, there will be no problems."

"It's just not like that, and you know it. Besides, maybe I don't really have good proof."

"Come on! The phone call last week is proof enough. *Ayman? How are his kidneys? What's the plan?* What about the fact that he makes you wear hijab around him now? And he's in America, but he walks around in a dishdasha all the time. Come on, Nur! He's practically the Taliban!" Elham exclaimed.

"Hey! That's my brother you're talking about!" Nur said hotly.

"Brother or not, that's how it is. You know the story of Ibrahim and his father in the Quran. You have to do what's right, even if it hurts your family. Now, give me the phone number you wrote down for the FBI. I'll call them."

When Saad heard that, he raised his eyebrows in shock and mouthed to his brother, "The FBI?"

"No, forget it."

"Nur, give it to me," Elham ordered.

"No, I said. Forget it!"

"Nur…"

"No!" Nur practically shouted.

"Fine. I'll just look it up on the internet, just like you did. I'm going to go call right now," Elham threatened.

"No, Elham, please! He's my brother!"

"Nur, don't be crazy! I have to!"

"Elham, you're my best friend. Please, please don't," Nur pleaded.

"Nur! He's working for Al Qaeda!"

Just then Saad burst into Nur's bedroom. Ibrahim wasn't far behind him.

"Nur, I have to tell you something," Saad said to her.

"Did you ever hear of knocking?" she retorted.

He ignored her. "I heard you talking the other night about how you went through my stuff, and I got upset. And all of this now, it's all an act. I didn't call Saudi Arabia last week. I called Khalid. And I don't care if you wear hijab around me or not. And the number for OL that you found is for Adnan's brother and his wife in Saudi Arabia," Saad told her.

"Oh. Okay," she said simply.

"Okay? That's it?"

She shrugged her shoulders. "Yeah, okay. So what do you want me to say?"

"Well… Oh, man! You knew!" he accused.

"Of course, I knew!" Nur exclaimed. "I mean, *Ayman*? Can you be any more obvious? Why didn't you just say hello, Osama? I mean, do you really expect me to believe that you can just pick up the phone and call Ayman whatever-his-name-is, just like that?"

"Man!" Saad shook his head in disbelief. "You annoying little brat! I should have known." He stormed out of the room. Ibrahim followed.

Nur turned to Elham. "We won," she said. "And that was really good about Prophet Ibrahim."

"It just came to me," Elham said modestly. "I didn't even think of it before when we were rehearsing. You were really good, too. In the end, the way you said, 'He's my brother!' That was really good."

"You think? I'm just glad to get back at Saad."

"Probably later you should talk to him," Elham said seriously. "Maybe he's a little upset."

"Well, it serves him right," Nur said unapologetically. "But I will. I'll talk to him tonight."

⌒

Later that evening, Nur knocked on Saad's closed bedroom door and then opened it a crack. "It's me," she said. "Can I come in?"

"I'm doing calculus," Saad said grouchily. He was sitting on the floor, books spread out around him.

Nur turned to Ibrahim, who was sitting at the desk, also doing homework. "Ibrahim, can I talk to Saad for a minute in private? Can you go in our room for a few minutes?" she requested.

He put down his pen. "Actually, I was going to use the computer anyway." He stood up and quietly left the room.

"What do you want?" Saad demanded.

Nur closed the door and sat down on the floor next to her brother. "I just want to say I'm sorry about everything," she apologized.

"Well, you should be."

"I mean, I'm sorry I accused you of changing. And I'm sorry I called your friends Wahabi. And I'm sorry I went through your stuff," she continued.

"That's all right," he said grudgingly.

"And I'm sorry I thought you were a terrorist."

Saad rolled his eyes. "Whatever. That's okay." He sighed. "But you need to be careful, Nur. Don't be like non-Muslims who accuse us of being terrorists based on nothing."

"I know. I hate it when people do that," she agreed.

"Maybe I am changing a little," Saad continued. "I don't want to forget Arabic, so I have been speaking it more. And I like Adnan and Yasser because they're religious, and they're really smart. I learn a lot from them. And I want to have a small beard. But none of this means I'm an extremist or a terrorist."

"I know." She looked down at the floor.

"Anyway, it's okay." He paused. "So you really thought I was too obvious? I mean, with the phone call? I thought I was doing a great acting job."

"Oh, man, it was so obvious," Nur declared. "I knew right away. Because you cannot just pick up the phone and call Ayman whatever-his-name-is just like that. I don't care if you're his son. I mean, the guy's in hiding. You have to use codes and… and puh-leese. How are his kidneys? Come on!"

"Yeah," he admitted. "I probably shouldn't have used the name Ayman. But what about the beard and the dishdasha and the sobha? Making Mom do stuff for me, all that?"

"Yeah, that was okay. I mean, you kind of did have me going there for a while," she agreed.

"Come on, admit it. I was a good actor, wasn't I?"

"Yeah," Nur gave in. "I mean, the way you went on and on about the bookstore being corrupt and all. And when you kept telling me to wear hijab around you, I almost started crying."

"Oh, I was serious about that," he said with a straight face.

For a second, she looked alarmed and instinctively reached up and grabbed her hair just as he added, "Just kidding."

"Ha, ha, ha." Nur didn't seem very amused. "Anyway, I just have a couple of questions. First of all, was that a real phone number and if it was, who is OL? And secondly—and I know I shouldn't have searched through your stuff—but anyway, what is this?" She handed him the piece of paper she had found in his pocket. "And my last question is why do you have a book on Arab nationalism?"

Saad glanced at the paper and then looked back at his sister. "Okay. First of all, OL is Adnan's brother Omar and his wife Latifa. I just jotted down the number in case Mom and Dad want it when they go to hajj this year. And secondly, that book I got from a friend who took a Middle Eastern history class last year. He said it was really good and informative. And the paper, I found inside the book. I must have just stuffed it in my pocket," he explained.

"Well, that makes sense. And that I believe, especially after looking through your pockets. You would not believe all of the stuff I found in there. I mean, your driver's license?"

"You went through my pockets?" he demanded incredulously.

"Well, uh…"

"Don't you ever go through my stuff again. Do you hear me?" Saad tried to sound threatening.

"Absolutely."

He sighed. "Good. Anything else?"

"Yeah. How were we? I mean, me and Elham? We really had you going, didn't we? I mean, you really thought we were going to call the FBI, didn't you?"

"You were okay," he hedged.

"Maybe I should be an actor, huh?" Nur persisted.

"Actually Elham was really good," Saad said. "You were okay, but Elham's the one who really made me think you were going to call the FBI."

"Well, I'll tell her that. Maybe she'll become an actress." Nur stood up. "I'll let you get back to your calculus now. Enjoy!"

Saad groaned. "Thanks," he said. "And thanks for stopping by."

"You're welcome. Bye." She left the room, closing the door behind her.

Chapter 16

AFTER THEIR QURAN CLASS that Saturday at the mosque, Ibrahim and his friends congregated in the library.

"Let's go to Farley Park," Ali suggested. "We can play basketball or soccer. It's so nice outside today."

"You guys go ahead," Ibrahim said. "I want to read for a few minutes and then I'll meet you there."

"Are you sure?" Khalid asked.

"Yeah, but can you maybe give Nur a ride home?" he requested. "We walked here, and I don't want her to have to walk home by herself."

"Sure, she can squeeze in the back with Elham and Hafsa."

"Yeah, 'cause I get the front," Farid spoke up. "I'm not allowed to sit next to Elham anymore."

"Why not?" Ibrahim asked curiously.

" Because the other day I had Hamid with me in the front and those two in the back. And all they did was fight and fight, like two little kids. And then Farid threw Elham's shoe out the window, and we had to stop and go back for it. And then I had to separate them, and put Hamid in the back and Elham in the front. I was so embarrassed," Khalid explained.

Ibrahim smiled. "I can't imagine Elham acting like that. Farid, yeah, but not Elham."

"Well, I think he started it," Khalid said.

"Hey!" Farid rebuked them.

"I heard my name," Elham said. "What's going on? What are you talking about?"

"About how you and Farid aren't allowed to sit next to each other in the car anymore," Ibrahim told her.

She groaned. "Don't remind me."

After the others took off, Ibrahim sat down on one of the couches and began reading the Quran. He had never really thought about it before, but reading the Quran was very relaxing. By the time he finally stopped, he felt so much stronger in his religion, and he knew that if he saw Christy at school on Monday, he had enough self-control that he would not go out with her again. He stood up and carried the Quran over to the bookshelf where it was kept. As he put it away, he heard someone coming down the stairs.

"I thought I heard someone down here," Imam Raheem said, once he reached the bottom. His two young sons were right behind him. "What are you still doing here, Ibrahim? Is everything okay?"

"Yeah, it's fine. I just wanted to read a little, that's all," Ibrahim replied.

"Well, I was getting ready to lock up. Did you want to stay longer?"

"No, I'm finished." He paused. "Um, Imam Raheem?"

"Yes?"

"In Islam, everything's forgiven, right? I mean, if you do something wrong and then really repent and change and stay with the religion, you're forgiven, right?"

"Well, yes, if you change from the heart. The Quran says in Sura Al-Nisa that if anyone does wrong or wrongs his soul, and then seeks forgiveness from Allah, he finds Allah most forgiving, most merciful. Is there something you want to talk about, Ibrahim jan?"

Ibrahim sighed. "No, thanks. I think I'm going to go. I'll let you get back home."

"I have plenty of time if you want to talk about something," Imam Raheem assured him.

"No, that's okay."

Ibrahim headed upstairs and out of the mosque. As he walked back toward his house, he thought seriously about what he needed to do. He was going to go home and change, and then go join his friends at Farley Park to play soccer. He needed to be with his friends, to relax with the guys, and have a good time before facing his parents with the truth, which he knew needed to be done. He wished he could erase the events of the past week. He felt so ashamed of everything he had done. But he vowed to change and to try not to do anything like that again.

⌒

"Mom, Dad, I need to talk to you," Ibrahim told his parents.

It was late Saturday night, after Nur and Mona had gone to sleep. Mr. and Mrs. Karim were watching television in the family room, waiting for Saad to come home from work. He was working until 11:00 that night.

Mr. Karim muted the television. "What's up?" he asked.

Ibrahim sat down in one of the chairs. "Well, I have a lot of things I need to tell you. And I just want to do it and get it over with, so…" He took a deep breath. "Okay. I lied to you this week. And I did some pretty bad stuff," he confessed.

His father turned off the television and looked at his son. "Go ahead."

"Well." He sighed. "This week, when I told you I was staying after school to be with my friends and stuff, I was actually going out with a girl."

"Oh?" Mrs. Karim said, raising her eyebrows.

"I'm really sorry about it," he said quickly. "I mean, I knew at the time that it was wrong, and I feel really bad about it. I just—"

"Did you do anything?" his mother asked.

"No," Ibrahim assured them. "No."

"Well, I don't know what to say. Ibrahim, I can't believe you would do this. You should know better. Why?"

"I don't know. I guess I thought it would be really cool to have a girlfriend. I just wanted to be like everyone else at school, you know, all the popular kids," he admitted.

"Does anyone else know about this?" Mrs. Karim asked.

Ibrahim shook his head. "No. I mean, I talked to Saad and Khalid about the idea, and both of them warned me not to go out with her. But they didn't know about this week."

"Well, good for them," Mr. Karim said. "It's really too bad you didn't listen."

Ibrahim sighed again. "Yeah."

"I don't know what to do about this," his father continued. "Ibrahim, we've always trusted you and tried to treat you like an adult. But now… You know, your mother and I have talked about what we would do if something like this were to happen with one of you. We planned that if it did, we would send you to live with your grandparents for a while, over in Jenin. But I didn't expect…" He let his words trail off.

"I think we need to talk about this a little," Mrs. Karim spoke up. "Ibrahim, why don't you go on to bed, and we'll talk to you in the morning."

"Are you serious?"

"Yes, your mother's right. We'll talk to you in the morning."

Ibrahim walked down the hallway to his bedroom. As he changed and brushed his teeth, he could hear his parents' whispered voices. He knew they were discussing his fate.

After a night of tossing and turning, Ibrahim woke up at around 5:30 AM and couldn't go back to sleep. He finally decided to go ahead and get up and pray. After washing up, he went out to the study where he prayed and then read for a while. After about twenty minutes, he went back to lie down for a little longer. He stayed in bed while he heard his parents rise to pray and start the day. He drifted off to sleep again for a while before waking about an hour later. Not able to take the suspense any longer, he decided to get up, take a shower, and find out his fate.

"I'll die if they send me to Jenin," Ibrahim said to himself while he showered. "Maybe I shouldn't have told them. Or maybe I just shouldn't have gone out with Christy to begin with," he thought ruefully.

When he finished his shower and emerged from the bathroom, he found his parents in the kitchen cooking breakfast together.

"*Sabah-al-khair*," he greeted them.

Mr. Karim was scrambling eggs at the stove. "*Sabah an-noor*," he replied.

"So, I can't take it any more," Ibrahim blurted out. "What are you going to do to me?"

"Well," his father began, "we talked quite a bit about it last night. You know, we had an hour while we were waiting for Saad. And anyway, we decided that you are almost an adult and you behaved like an adult. You did something wrong. You knew it was wrong, but you did it anyway. And you lied to us. But then you came forward and told us the truth."

"So, it's only fair that we treat you like an adult, too," Mrs. Karim put in.

"So we're not going to punish you," her husband said.

"What?" Ibrahim couldn't believe what he had just heard.

"That's right," his mother agreed. "But there's a couple of things we need to make clear. This doesn't mean you're getting off free. If something like this happens again, even if you come forward and tell us, you will definitely be going to Jenin for a few months. We even talked to your grandparents last night."

"And for the next two months, until you prove to us that we can trust you again, the only person you can go out with will be Khalid or Hamid. And if you do go out with one of them, expect that we will be calling to make sure you are there," Mr. Karim added. "But the most important thing now is that what you did was very wrong, and you knew it was wrong, but you did it anyway. And this is very bad for you. So you need to really start trying to do better. You don't just have to prove yourself to us. Most importantly, you have to prove yourself to Allah."

"I know," Ibrahim assured them. "I will."

Chapter 17

MONDAY MORNING ELHAM HAD JUST walked out of her English class when she heard an unfamiliar voice behind her.

"Elham!" someone was calling.

Elham cautiously looked over her shoulder as scenes from the incident two weeks ago flashed through her mind. Beth was walking briskly to catch up with her. She sighed with relief.

"Beth," Elham said, pausing to wait for her. "I saw you in class. I can't believe you came today."

"Yeah." Beth sighed as the two girls began walking together.

"Oh, come on. It's not that bad," Elham chided.

"Says who?" Beth retorted. "I hate science. And I don't know what the point of pre-algebra is besides torture."

Elham groaned. "If you don't like algebra, wait until you take geometry. I hate geometry, but I thought algebra was fun."

"For a nerd," Beth teased.

Elham laughed and rolled her eyes as they stopped at her locker. "I'm not a nerd. Hey, are you going to lunch now?"

"Yeah."

"Do you want to sit with me and my friends?" she invited.

"Uh…"

"Oh, you'll love them," Elham insisted as she traded books. "My friend Hafsa is so sweet. And Kate is her best friend. She's really nice. Plus Alexis, who's in our science class—well, my science class—but she has Mrs. Falls, too."

"Well, maybe," Beth agreed hesitantly.

Elham closed her locker. "Come on. There's Alexis."

They hurried to catch up with the blonde-haired teenager.

"Hey, Alexis. Beth, this is Alexis. Alexis, this is Beth," Elham introduced the girls. "Alexis is in my science class. And Beth has Mrs. Falls, too. She has it with Ali." She turned to Beth. "Do you know Ali? His sister is Nadia, one of my best friends. We don't let Alexis hang out with Nadia and Ali 'cause then they speak Bosnian, and we can't understand them."

"It's Serbo-Croatian," Alexis corrected as they headed toward the cafeteria. "And we only speak in it when we talk about you."

"Funny," Elham retorted.

"You guys seem really smart," Beth said.

"Elham is. She's, like, the smartest girl in our class," Alexis replied. "But I'm not. The only class I like is art."

"I like art, too," Beth agreed.

"That's good. And you said you didn't like anything about school," Elham reminded her.

"Well…"

"I always wished I could draw," Elham interrupted before she could add something negative.

"All Elham can draw is stick figures," Alexis teased as they joined their other friends at a table.

"But I draw them really good," she retorted.

Alexis turned back to Beth. "So what kind of art do you like?"

Elham smiled. It was great to see Alexis and Beth get along. She pulled out her lunch—a veggie burger and an apple—and began talking to Hafsa and Kate.

⌐

After school that day, Khalid was hanging out with Ibrahim and Mark at Ibrahim's locker.

"Great game this weekend," Khalid told them.

"Ali's getting to be a really good goalie," Mark agreed. "Do you think coach will let him play more next year?"

"Probably," Khalid said. "I mean, he was just a freshman this year."

"When are you going to cut your hair?" Ibrahim asked Mark.

Mark's blond hair had grown to about shoulder length. He kept it pulled back in a ponytail. "You sound like my mom," he retorted.

"I was just wondering. Are you going to be like one of those eccentric geniuses?" Ibrahim teased.

"All professional soccer players have their signature hair style," his friend replied.

Just then Ibrahim noticed Christy heading toward them. She was holding hands with a dark-haired boy.

"Hi, Ibrahim," she greeted him. "This is Daniel. He's a junior. We hooked up at the party this weekend. The one you didn't go to because you were hanging out with your parents." She smiled with a hint of a smirk.

"Hi," Ibrahim said simply.

"What's up?" Daniel replied, putting his arm around Christy's waist.

"Daniel's a wrestler. He was ninth in the state last year, and he was only a sophomore," Christy said proudly, patting him on the arm. "This year I bet he'll be first."

"Congratulations," Ibrahim said.

"Thanks."

"Ibrahim's in my biology class. He plays soccer," Christy told her new boyfriend. She giggled. "Did you even know we have a soccer team? I don't even know what happens in a soccer game."

"I thought only girls played soccer," Daniel remarked.

"I think it's the most popular sport in the world, for men and women," Ibrahim replied.

"But not in America," Daniel pointed out.

"Ibrahim's Muslim," Christy piped up.

Her new boyfriend smirked. "Really?"

Ibrahim flushed.

Mark jumped to his rescue. "Germany won the last men's soccer World Cup. That's Germany, the country. You know, in Asia."

"Of course, I know where it is," Daniel said defensively as Mark held back a smile.

"Come on, Danny, let's go." Christy pulled at his arm.

"Great idea." They started to walk away. "No one plays soccer," Daniel added. "Hey, sweetie, how about a kiss?"

"Gross," Khalid said after they left.

"I can't believe you went out with her, and *I* told you to," Mark added. "How many guys has she been with anyway?"

"I don't know. Probably a lot. But she's okay. It's her parents' fault. They don't care what she does. When I went to her house, her mom had left a message saying they were in Kansas City and wouldn't be back until late and for her and her brother to leave a note if they went out."

"Wow," Mark said. "My parents have to know every detail of my schedule. Who I'm going out with and where we'll be and what we'll be doing. They would never be like that."

"Tell me about it," Ibrahim agreed.

"Well, you guys. I need to get going. Elham and Hafsa are probably waiting for me," Khalid announced.

"I'll walk with you," Ibrahim said. "Maybe I'll find Nur with them. See ya, Mark."

"Bye."

"I can't believe that's what I wanted," Ibrahim said as they walked away. "I really wanted to be seen with her in school, holding her hand, even kissing her. Showing everyone that she was my girlfriend."

"Yeah, well, we all make mistakes," Khalid said.

"Yeah. Thanks for everything, man."

"No problem."

"Say, Khalid, how long have we known each other?" Ibrahim asked.

"Since junior high, so…. what? Four years," Khalid answered. "Why?"

"And you still wear that shirt."

Khalid glanced down at his t-shirt. "What's wrong with it? It was big when I got it in seventh grade. Now it fits."

"But it's so out."

"It's Fido. Fido is never out," Khalid said defensively.

"Well, I hate to tell you this, but Fido was out before you even got the shirt," Ibrahim laughed.

"My parents got me this shirt," his friend replied.

Ibrahim smiled. "Cute. There's Nur and Hamid. I'll see you later, Khalid." He headed over to where his sister and friend were waiting for him.

Chapter 18

"HERE WE ARE AGAIN," Nadia said philosophically. "Another Saturday after class." She was sitting with Nur and Elham in Elham's bedroom late Saturday afternoon.

"You know," Elham said, "I feel like I've grown up a lot in the last few weeks."

"I know," Nur agreed.

"So, I keep forgetting to ask you." Nadia turned to Elham. "Did you end up calling that girl?"

"Yes, I did," Elham answered. "I can't believe I forgot to tell you guys. I did call her last Friday night. And when she answered, she didn't really want to talk. So I asked her to meet me Saturday morning at Sabrina's. And she said no, but then I went there anyway, and after a while she came."

"Huh."

"Yeah. And actually she had something really interesting to say which I never thought about before. I mean, initially she said the reason that she did what she did to me and then Khalid and my family was because she hates Muslims. But when I pushed her on it, she said that actually it was because she thinks we're really exclusive. You know, we just hang out with each other. You know, with other Muslims," Elham told them. "And I never really thought about it before, but she's right."

"Because a lot of people don't like us, so it's easier," Nur said.

"Well, that's what I said. But then she said that maybe if we weren't so exclusive, stuff like this wouldn't happen," Elham added.

"Hmm. Wow. You know, I never really thought about, but she has a good point," Nadia agreed.

"Yeah, I think so," Nur added. "Because when you're exclusive, people think you're acting high when you're really not."

"Anyway, so I've talked to her a few times this week, and I gave her my phone number, so hopefully she'll call. You know, the other day when I was talking to her… I just feel so bad for her," Elham said. "She doesn't even know her dad. And I guess her mom lives somewhere else and does drugs and stuff. She lives with her grandparents. And she's always skipping school. I'm really glad she decided to come back to school, at least for right now."

"That's so sad." Nadia sounded genuinely sympathetic. "Why don't you invite her here? I'll do her hair."

"You just want to do her hair," Nur teased. It was no secret that Nadia's goal was to be a hair stylist.

"Anyway," Nadia said, trying to change the subject. "We probably need to try to be friends with more non-Muslims."

"Yeah, that's my goal," Elham agreed. "And, actually, I already started. Remember I told you about Maria, the Spanish girl in my science class? She's from Guatemala, not Mexico. Anyway, her parents have a Spanish grocery store downtown, and she works there sometimes to help them. And she said Sundays are usually pretty slow and boring, so I told her I would stop by tomorrow to say hi."

"That'll be nice," Nadia said.

"Yeah, I'm excited." She was quiet for a minute. "Anyway, that's not the only thing I have to tell you guys. Guess what else happened last Friday?"

"What?" Nur demanded.

"The FBI called my dad," she told them dramatically. "They wanted to interview him, so he went there Monday."

"Why?" Nur asked.

"Well, apparently Mr. Kinzey must have called them, because I guess they had copies of those papers from the AIO about Muslims in America—the one that also has information about Muslims in Iowa. And that's one of the papers that my dad gave him when he and the Azizis went to meet with him." The Azizis were the young couple from the mosque. "Anyway, he had the interview yesterday, and they were asking him about contacts with the AIO because I guess they think the AIO supports terrorism."

"Are you serious?" Nadia sounded incredulous.

"Yeah. Can you believe it? The AIO?"

"I can't believe Mr. Kinzey. I mean, just because your dad wanted to educate him about Islam a little, he goes and calls the FBI? That's crazy!" Nadia shook her head in disbelief.

"I know," Elham agreed. "So what do you expect from his students? Or his teachers?"

"Maybe he gave it to Mrs. Falls, and she called the FBI," Nur suggested.

"I don't know. He didn't go back and ask Mr. Kinzey about it," Elham said.

"Maybe he should have," Nur said. "Mr. Kinzey doesn't seem like he would do something like that. I know he wasn't that helpful when your dad met him, but I still don't think that he would call the FBI just because they wanted to talk to him about Islam."

"Actually, they also called Khalil Azizi, you know, from the mosque. He and his wife went with my dad to talk to Mr. Kinzey."

"Isn't it ironic how Monday afternoon we were pretending to call the FBI at the same time that your dad was actually talking to them?" Nur added.

"Except we weren't actually going to call them," Elham reminded her.

"I know. And I apologized to Saad that night. And, by the way, I forgot to tell you that he said you're a good actress," Nur told her friend.

"How could you forget to tell me something like that?"

Nur shrugged her shoulders. "I don't know. Actually he said I was okay, but you were the one who convinced him that we were really serious."

"Wow, what a compliment!"

"Yeah, I told you that line about Prophet Ibrahim was really good."

"I still can't believe you guys actually did that," Nadia said, shaking her head.

"Hey, he deserved it. You weren't there. You have no idea how mean he was to me," Nur said defensively.

Nadia rolled her eyes. "Whatever. I'm just glad you apologized."

⌐

Meanwhile, across the street at the Karims, their four brothers were hanging out in the partially-finished basement. Saad was at work.

"Man, I am so tired," Khalid said. "I had to work at 6:00 AM this morning."

"Why'd you work so early?" Ibrahim asked.

"I usually work early on Sundays, and they asked me to work early today, too. I don't mind it. Usually after I finish, I go home and take a nap, and then I still have the rest of the day to finish my homework. And since today's Saturday, I have the rest of the day for myself."

Ali groaned. "Don't remind me about homework. I have another history test on Monday."

"So what was it like going out with a girl?" Farid asked.

"What do you think?" Ibrahim shot back. "It was haram. Of course, it was nice, too. That's one of the reasons why it's haram. Because it's so nice, it's too hard to stop with just holding hands or kissing a little. It's just too tempting, so it has to be haram."

"Wow, that's pretty deep," Khalid remarked.

"Yeah, well, supposedly your mistakes make you a better person, right?" Ibrahim sighed.

"I can't believe you told your parents," Ali said. "I would be afraid to."

"Well, I had to. I felt so guilty about it."

"You're really lucky they didn't do anything," Khalid said. "I'm sure my dad would have been furious."

"I think parents are okay sometimes," Ibrahim replied. "I mean, I think they were really glad that I did tell them. They said that that's the reason they decided not to send me over to live with my grandparents in Jenin… because I felt so guilty, and I came forward, and admitted what I did. I couldn't believe it. I thought for sure they wouldn't let me leave the house again."

"It might have been easier if they *had* sent you over to Jenin," Farid spoke up. "I mean, it's so much easier to be a good Muslim and stay with the religion over there than it is here. There's too many temptations here."

"That's what makes you a better Muslim. Besides, they might not have all the temptations, but they have their problems, too," his older brother argued. "Their lives are so hard. People die from hunger and poverty and violence every day there, and they still practice their faith and stay strong with Islam. And here, it's the opposite. Our lives are so easy, but we have all these temptations. So we still need to practice our faith and stay strong with Islam."

"Wow, I didn't know my brother was so smart," Farid said. "That's really deep."

"He's right, though," Ibrahim added. "We do need to stay strong with Islam. We can't give in to temptations like I did last week. I still feel so guilty about it. I feel like I won't ever make it up with Allah."

"It's okay," Khalid reassured him. "People make mistakes. Allah understands. It's just like what you said before. It's what you do after the mistakes that counts the most."

Ibrahim sighed. "You're right," he agreed. "And I will never do anything like that again."

"I still can't believe Nur actually thought that Saad was becoming a terrorist," Farid remarked. "And I feel so embarrassed that Elham did, too."

Ibrahim groaned. "Don't remind me. That was a mess."

Ali laughed. "Did Saad actually go to class wearing his dishdasha?" he wanted to know.

"No, he took it off as soon as he got out of the neighborhood," Ibrahim told them. "He didn't even wait until he got to school. He said with his luck, if he left it on, that would be the one day that he got a speeding ticket or something."

"Wouldn't that be funny?" Farid added. "Imagine what the police would think."

"They'd probably arrest him," Khalid said soberly. "I lectured Elham about it the other day because she shouldn't have been so judgmental."

"Hey, enough of this," Farid interrupted. "Let's have some fun. There's no girls down here. It's just us and the ping pong table. Who wants to go first?" He grabbed a paddle from the table. "Come on, don't be afraid."

"You're the one who should be afraid," Ibrahim warned him as he picked up another paddle and quickly headed over to the other side.

Upstairs, Mr. Karim had paused by the open basement door on his way out of the kitchen. He walked into the family room and sat down on the couch next to his wife. "You know, we've got some good kids," he told her.

She looked up at him from the newspaper and smiled. "I know."

About the Author

Maryam Mahmoodian is a second generation Muslim-American, born and raised in the U.S. Her father is from Iran, and her mother is American. She grew up reading such series as Nancy Drew and Trixie Belden. This is her first published book. She is currently a family physician in Lincoln, Nebraska, where she lives with her husband.

Another quality Islamic Fiction book published by
Muslim Writers Publishing

Sophia's Journal: Time Warp 1857

Author, Najiyah Helwani

During a bike ride with her family near Lawrence, Kansas, anxiety-ridden Sophia falls into a river and is washed downstream. She emerges in 1857 – smack in the middle of Bleeding Kansas. Sophia is aghast to find that slavery is going on in her adopted community, and she and begins to fight for the freedom of the slaves she knows. A local boy captures Sophia's heart, but when he proposes marriage, Sophia is torn about marrying outside her faith. An old Gambian slave, who is still a closet Muslim, helps her work out her fears, and this causes an exciting, dangerous and unexpected turn of events.

The author researched historical types of food, clothing and the way of life in 1857 Kansas, USA. Readers will love learning about the way of life early frontier settlers lived. The book has a glossary and some unique recipes that are specific to the book's period in history. This book will be a welcome addition to any Language Arts reading and/or American History program.

Islamic Fiction Books

Muslim Writers Publishing is proud to have published *Muslim Teens in Pitfalls and Pranks*, a quality Islamic Fiction book for teens and young adults. You can learn more about the availability of Islamic Fiction books and Muslim authors by visiting: www. IslamicFictionBooks.com

Islamic Fiction books: This refers to creative, imaginative fiction books written by Muslims and marketed primarily to Muslims. Islamic Fiction may be marketed to secular markets, too. The content of these books incorporates some religious content and themes, and may include non-fictionalized historical or factual Islamic content with or without direct reference to the Qur'an or the Sunnah of the Prophet (pbuh). The stories may also include modern, real life situations and moral dilemmas. Islamic Fiction may be written in many languages. Islamic Fiction books do not include any of the following Harmful Content:

- vulgar language
- sexually explicit content
- un-Islamic practices that are not identified as un-Islamic
- content that portrays Islam in a negative way

Linda D. Delgado, Publisher
Muslim Writers Publishing

Muslim Writers Publishing Books
Available at www.MuslimWritersPublishing.com

Islamic Fiction Titles

Muslim Teens in Pitfalls and Pranks by Maryam Mahmoodian
The Runaway Scarf by Corey Habbas
Sophia's Journal: Time Warp 1857 by Najiyah Diana Helwani
The Size of a Mustard Seed by Umm Juwayriyah
    (Forthcoming Summer - 2008)
The Gift by Zaipah Ibrahim (Forthcoming Summer - 2008)

Islamic Rose Books series 1: *The Visitors* by Linda D. Delgado
Islamic Rose Books series 2: *Hijab-Ez Friends* by Linda D. Delgado
Islamic Rose Books series 3: *Stories* by Linda D. Delgado
Islamic Rose Books series 4: *Saying Goodbye* by Linda D. Delgado

Echoes series 1: *Echoes* by Jamilah Kolocotronis
Echoes series 2: *Rebounding* by Jamilah Kolocotronis
Echoes series 3: *Turbulence* by Jamilah Kolocotronis
Echoes series 4: *Ripples* by Jamilah Kolocotronis
    (Forthcoming Summer - 2008)

Non-fiction Titles

Power Poetry for Wide Awake Youth by Habibullah Saleem
Star Writers by Amatullah Al-Marwani
The Beautiful Names by Saaleha E. Bhamjee
    (Forthcoming Spring - 2008)
A Muslim's Guide to Publishing and Marketing by Linda D. Delgado
Halal Food, Fun, and Laughter by Linda D. Delgado

Lightning Source UK Ltd.
Milton Keynes UK
UKOW051944130213

206258UK00001B/111/P